Battle Hymn

by Jim Leonard

A SAMUEL FRENCH ACTING EDITION

SAMUEL FRENCH

FOUNDED 1830

NEW YORK HOLLYWOOD LONDON TORONTO

SAMUELFRENCH.COM

ISBN 978-0-573-60094-4   Printed in U.S.A.   #29735

MUSIC MATERIALS

Music materials consisting of a **Rehearsal CD, a Performance CD, and Music Lead Sheets** will be loaned two months prior to the production ONLY on the receipt of the Licensing Fee quoted for all performances, and an additional materials fee.

Please contact Samuel French for perusal of the music materials as well as a performance license application.

IMPORTANT BILLING AND CREDIT
REQUIREMENTS

All producers of *BATTLE HYMN* must give credit to the Author of the Play in all programs distributed in connection with performances of the Play, and in all instances in which the title of the Play appears for the purposes of advertising, publicizing or otherwise exploiting the Play and/or a production. The name of the Author *must* appear on a separate line on which no other name appears, immediately following the title and *must* appear in size of type not less than fifty percent of the size of the title type.

BATTLE HYMN was first produced by Circle X Theatre (Tim Wright, Artistic Director) at [Inside] the Ford Theatre in Los Angeles on January 17, 2009. The performance was directed by John Langs, with sets and lighting by Brian Sidney Bembridge, costumes by Dianne K. Graebner, sound by Cricket S. Myers, properties by Ali Hisserich, makeup and hair by Emily McDonald, scenic painting by Jen Kays and Lauren Horowitz, and an original score by Michael Levine. The production stage manager was Kathleen Ressegger, assisted by Cate Cundiff, and the play featured projections by Jason H. Thompson, assisted by Matthew Melinger. The play was produced by Tim Wright and Jennifer A. Skinner. Associate producers were Camille Schenkkan and Jen Kays. The cast was as follows:

MARTHA . . . . Suzy Jane Hunt

MAN ONE: HENRY, CONDUCTOR, FARMER, REB, CALF,
    VIRGIN MARY, STEWARDESS, HANK . . . . Bill Heck

MAN TWO: AMBROSE, SOLDIER #1, GUARD, MOTHER COW,
    KLINGGINHOFFER, MARK, FLOWER, DOCTOR . . . . William Salyers

MAN THREE: WILLARD, DANTE, COW, SOLDIER #2, LANFORD,
    PSYCHIATRIC AIDE, BARKER, BETTY . . . . Robert Manning, Jr.

MAN FOUR: PRIMBODY, SGT. MCMURPHY, ONE-LEGGED OFFICER,
    SLAVE, NURSE SINGER, SADIE, ADMINISTRATOR,
    SUNSHINE . . . . John Short

CHARACTERS

This play is performed by one woman and four men.

MARTHA –16

MAN ONE plays: HENRY, CONDUCTOR, FARMER, REB, CALF, VIRGIN MARY, STEWARDESS, HANK

MAN TWO plays: AMBROSE, SOLDIER #1, GUARD, MOTHER COW, KLING-GINHOFFER, MARK, FLOWER, DOCTOR

MAN THREE plays: WILLARD, DANTE, COW, SOLDIER #2, LANFORD, PSY-CHIATRIC AIDE, BARKER, BETTY

MAN FOUR plays: MR. PRIMBODY, SGT. MCMURPHY, ONE-LEGGED OFFICER, SLAVE, NURSE SINGER, SADIE, ADMINISTRATOR, SUNSHINE

SETTING

A raked, wooden stage. A raised platform or "bridge" upstage would be nice. We need to be able to project images on the upstage wall. Furniture is brought on when needed, but should be bare-bones. A huge, battle-worn American flag might serve as the curtain.

COSTUMES

The men require numerous changes, many of which have to be quick changes. Perhaps the "key" to realizing these costumes is the cows. When Man Three plays a Cow in the first act, he should have some white make-up around one eye, and be dressed in dark, raggedy clothing, with an old cow bell around his neck. Mother Cow should be dressed in a brown and white cow-patterned, long skirt, a brown blouse, and a bonnet with cow-pattern. She wears cow bell. Her Calf should be dressed in cow-patterned overalls that match his mother, and he, too, has a cow bell. All the cows are bare-footed. Keep it simple, iconic.

A NOTE ABOUT LANGUAGE

The playwright has chosen his curse words with care; however, if producers finds the play too racy, they may substitute less racy language where appropriate. Caution: this does not mean producers have permission to cut the "gay" out of this play.

ACKNOWLEDGEMENTS

Battle Hymn was developed with steadfast support from the New Harmony Project. The play then received a development workshop from the University of Evansville Theatre Department, produced by John David Lutz and directed by Scott R. Lank; they put my play on its feet, and helped me discover the arc of the story. Circle X Theatre gave the script a rehearsed reading in Los Angeles, under the direction of John Langs. Circle X encouraged me to continue writing, thinking, trying, failing, flailing, and discovering the characters and story arcs throughout the brilliant madness of rehearsals and well into our award-winning run. I could not have created *Battle Hymn* without them.

– Jim Leonard

For Linda, the love of my life,

and mother to our beautiful sons, Abel and Grayston.

ACT ONE: THIS WORLD

(Music. A dreamy, strange waltz. **MARTHA** *enters to find* **FOUR MEN** *onstage, dressed in the uniform of their local militia, circa 1861 – A bright maroon coat with a high collar, a sash, possibly a scabbard. Note: the uniform isn't ridiculous, it's just trying a little too hard. The men face upstage with their backs to the audience.)*

*(***MARTHA*** "wolf" whistles at* **HENRY** *when she sees him. He turns to her and bows deeply. He's proud of himself.)*

HENRY. Good evening, Miss Martha.

MARTHA. Why, good heavens, Henry! You look so –

HENRY. *(pleased)* I do, don't I?

MARTHA. You are really –

HENRY. I know it – I really am.

MARTHA. You are just –

HENRY. You don't have to tell me – I know! The Ladies Auxilary sewed uniforms for all the boys in the Home Militia, but I have to admit mine fits me.

MARTHA. It really does.

HENRY. We elected officers and everything. Plus, we named ourselves. We voted. Unanimous and democratic. We're called the Brave Sons of Kentucky.

(beat)

I like your dress.

(Beat. They've run out of conversation.)

MARTHA. The music's sure pretty.

HENRY. You want to dance.

MARTHA. *(pleased)* I'd be honored to, Henry.

HENRY. Not with me. I don't know how.

MARTHA. You can do it. Just take my hand.

HENRY. Well. OK.

MARTHA. Put that hand on my waist.

(He does.)

And get a feeling for the music.

HENRY. *(in time to the music)* Feel –

MARTHA. Feel –

HENRY. Feel –

MARTHA. Go.

> *(They dance. A little hesitant at first, but in a heart-breaking, innocent, earnest way. Within moments, they're actually waltzing together in a rudimentary, romantic fashion.)*
>
> *(As they dance, the* **OTHER MILITIA MEMBERS** *begin dancing, too; only they have imaginary partners.* **MARTHA** *is the only girl in the world. After fifteen or twenty seconds of waltzing,* **MARTHA** *spins away from* **HENRY** *and into a special.)*

MARTHA. *(to the theatre)* I fell for Henry Tall the first time I laid eyes on him.

> *(The* **WALTZING MEN** *may continue behind her, but in relief/silhouette now…stylized. Focus is all on her.)*

It was the first day of school, and I was sitting off by myself on the rope swing at recess, when Henry comes striding right over, points, and, says, "Hey." Just like that –

> *(***HENRY***, indeed, walks up and says:)*

HENRY. Hey. You want a push?

MARTHA. Well, I looked in his blue, blue, blue eyes and I felt like the whole sky was opening. As if gravity had no hold on me whatsoever. Then I felt his finger tips brush against my bottom…

> *(***HENRY*** *mimes pulling her back and letting go. She 'swings' gloriously.)*

HENRY. Wanna go higher?

MARTHA. Yes!

HENRY. Higher?

MARTHA. Way higher!

(*HENRY pushes as if he's running under the mimed 'swing,' then rejoins the stylized waltz of his fellow militia men.*)

(*to the theatre*)

I can still feel the wind on my face and the sky flying up and out between my legs. I clearly remember saying to myself, "Tomorrow I ain't gonna wear any underwear."

(*then*)

I spent the rest of my life trying to making Henry Tall like me. I never told him, of course, but I used to write poems to that boy, which I cried over, and secretly burned. When I took a bath, I pretended he was the soap and I was the wash cloth. My hands were his hands whenever I touched me, and Lord knows I touched myself all the time.

(*MARTHA looks at HENRY, feeling too many feelings:*)

Now he's joined up to fight in a stupid ole war, and I'm so tore up I could spit rusty nails. But at least Henry's asked me to dance.

(*HENRY holds out his hand in mid-turn and twirls her into the waltz. They dance beautifully now, as the other MEN dance/filter off stage. MARTHA and HENRY end up in a striking pose, just as the song ends.*)

(*She pushes him.*)

You out and out fibbed to me, Henry! You do too know how to dance!

HENRY. I don't! I really don't! I swear I never danced once in my life till just now.

MARTHA. I'll be dogged.

HENRY. We make pretty good partners, huh?

MARTHA. Hey, Henry?

HENRY. Yeah?

MARTHA. You want to walk me home?

HENRY. Sure.

(*She takes his arm; they cross; a full moon fills the sky.*)

MARTHA. Time goes so fast. I just can't believe you're leaving tomorrow.

HENRY. It's really too bad you're a girl. I wish you had the opportunity to come along with us. We are gonna march ourselves to victory!

MARTHA. I may never see you again.

HENRY. Oh, Lord love a goose, Martha, don't talk like that!

MARTHA. You'll write to me, won't you?

HENRY. I don't expect I'll have much time for correspondence, what with all the battles and everything.

MARTHA. I'm gonna wait for you, Henry. I miss you already.

HENRY. Gosh, I wish you were a boy. Wait'll you see us all snapping in out of attention –

MARTHA. Henry?

HENRY. Yeah?

MARTHA. You have my permission to kiss me if you'd like.

HENRY. What do you mean?

MARTHA. (*almost welling with tears*) I've just liked you so much for so long...what if you get wounded? Or worse?

HENRY. Shoot, I'll be home before harvest time.

MARTHA. You just come back in one piece, you hear?

(*She kisses his cheek. Beat. They hesitate, then kiss on the lips. They stop for a moment, and now he takes her in his arms, and they kiss with passion. Then...*)

Henry?

HENRY. (*nervous*) Yeah? What? Did I do something wrong?

MARTHA. No! No, I just...

HENRY. Because I never...you know –

MARTHA. I never neither.

HENRY. *(relieved)* Really?

MARTHA. You truly are something all gussied up like that.

HENRY. I hate to brag on myself, but I do feel sharp as a stick.

MARTHA. *(level)* Take it off.

(Sound of distant drums begins in the background.)

HENRY. What do you mean?

*(**MARTHA** begins undoing his buttons.)*

Lord love a goose.

MARTHA. Promise you'll never forget me.

HENRY. I won't.

MARTHA. You better not, Henry.

HENRY. Oh, boy…oh, God…

(She pulls him upstage, kisses him passionately, and the drums grow much louder, building to a cannon-like clap.)

*(Special on **REVEREND AMBROSE WATERS** praying on his knees, downstage. He's wearing a long nightshirt, a robe, and slippers. He has a hint of a well-bred Eastern accent. **SERVANTS** have brought on a long, elegant breakfast table. **WILLARD**, a black man, is his butler. **WILLARD** is lit in silhouette until he speaks.)*

AMBROSE. Oh, God – dear, dear God – my life has been wrecked upon the rocky shoals! Sixteen long years I have labored here, Lord. Sixteen long years I have preached your holy word to these backwater heathens. And what do I have to show for it? I have found hell and it's name is Kentucky! I matriculated Harvard at the top of my class. I could have gone to India.

WILLARD. India, Reverend?

*(**AMBROSE** rises from his knees, and "enters" the scene.)*

AMBROSE. India! Asia! The Orient, yes! But, no, Willard – no, no, no, no! I chose to evangelize this miscreant, tobacco stained land. Oh, I had dreams when I came here. Visions, I tell you! A shining congregation in the midst this tree-shrouded dungeon. A beacon of civilized humanity to light the way West! And what is my reward for my life's work to be? Fully half my congregation has gone to war, Willard! My deacons forsake me. My Choir Master has taken up arms against my Sunday School teacher, whom he claims is a Yankee. They are fist fighting and dueling each other in the church yard. Have I taught these people nothing? I tell you, the devil has afflicted this country with war fever, Willard – the hoary finger of Satan himself is poised upon the trigger!

WILLARD. You'll feel better when you eat some eggs, Reverend.

AMBROSE. I don't deserve to be fed, I deserve to be flogged! How could I be so blind?

*(**MARTHA** enters.)*

MARTHA. Good morning.

AMBROSE. Good morning.

WILLARD. Good morning.

MARTHA. Good morning.

AMBROSE. *(They do this every morning.)* Romans! Chapter three, verse twenty-three!

MARTHA. "For all have sinned, and come short of the glory of God."

AMBROSE. Did you sleep well? I'm starving.

WILLARD. Eggs, Miss Martha?

MARTHA. My stomach's in more of a dry toast formation, thank you, Willard.

AMBROSE. Your mother, God rest her soul, she used to say that a good hearty breakfast is the key to a productive day.

(a quick prayer:)

God bless these scrambled eggs to our bodies, and us to the use of the Savior.

AMBROSE & WILLARD & MARTHA. Amen.

MARTHA. Willard, I need to speak to my father privately.

WILLARD. I'll see to the kitchen.

(He exits.)

AMBROSE. Good man, that boy. We're lucky to have him.

MARTHA. Pa, I want to get married. To Henry.

AMBROSE. Henry the Tall boy?

MARTHA. I know you don't like him because he's a Baptist and we're Episcopalians, but –

AMBROSE. Denomination has nothing to do with it, Martha. I'm ecumenical at core. If and when this dreadful Rebellion is settled, and if and when Henry returns, then we can revisit the idea of my only child betrothing herself to an uneducated farmer who speaks in tongues and handles snakes.

MARTHA. I'm having his baby.

AMBROSE. Oh, sweet God.

MARTHA. What with you being a minister, Pa, maybe you could help me and Henry get married, even though we're not in the same exact...state. Can somebody marry somebody who's not in the same place? I know! What if we write him a letter and do it by post? Then I'll put a ring on and he'll put a ring on, and then we'll be legal. In the eyes of the Lord, I mean. Cause that's real important to me.

*(**AMBROSE** picks up a small silver bell from the table and rings it.)*

*(**MARTHA** continues on in a rush of emotion:)*

MARTHA. *(cont.)* Henry loves me. I love him. I love you. And the more I think about being a mama, the more overjoyed I get. I just feel so different. So older. So, I don't know...*life!* I don't even mind up-chucking, Pa. I've got a whole nother person inside me. I'm two people at once. I'm having a baby. We're having a baby.

AMBROSE. You have ruined both of our lives. Do you comprehend that?

WILLARD. *(enters)* You rang?

AMBROSE. Willard. Please pack my daughter's belongings immediately.

WILLARD. Is Miss Martha going somewhere?

AMBROSE. *(sharp)* Do as I say, Willard. Thank you.

(**WILLARD** *exits.*)

I came out West to evangelize the heathens, and they have evangelized you.

MARTHA. Pa, I don't want to leave you.

AMBROSE. You will take the first train to Philadelphia. I will wire my sister. You will remain in her care until after this…bastard is born. You will then give the child away to an appropriate Christian institution.

(then)

I trust you understand the utmost discretion is an absolute necessity.

MARTHA. I trust you understand that I hate you completely.

AMBROSE. Martha, a girl in your condition is much like a horse without legs. You are mired and crippled in sin!

MARTHA. I want to keep my baby.

AMBROSE. What you want and what you do will not remain synonymous, Martha! What does God say about harlotry? Hebrews. Chapter 13. Verse 4.

MARTHA. I'm not a harlot – I'm your daughter.

AMBROSE. How will God judge you? Where will God judge you? Do you think you can escape His wrath? Hebrews 13:4. What does the Bible say?

MARTHA. I don't care what it says!

(He slaps her hard across the face. Then says softly:)

AMBROSE. "Whores and adulterers will be judged in hell." Good bye, Martha.

(A screaming train whistle as the lights change. The **CONDUCTOR** *is played by the same actor who played* **HENRY.***)*

CONDUCTOR. All aboard!

(Music...

(The **MEN** *strike the table. The chairs become seats on the train.)*

(Lights rise on **MARTHA** *with a carpet bag. The faint sound of rails clickety-clacking below us wouldn't hurt a thing.* **MARTHA** *stands in front of two sleeping men:* **MR. PRIMBODY;** *and* **DANTE,** *who is played the same actor who played* **WILLARD.***)*

MARTHA. Excuse me. Sir? 'scuse me, please.

*(***PRIMBODY*** awakes. He's a backwoods Southern dandy.)*

MR. PRIMBODY. What? What? What? What?

MARTHA. I believe you're in my seat, sir.

MR. PRIMBODY. Oh, me, oh, my. As the French say, pardon me. Might I be of help with your luggage?

MARTHA. Why, thank you.

MR. PRIMBODY. Percival D. Primbody at your service. Is it Madam or Miss? No, no, don't tell me. Allow me to hazard a guess. You're uhhh...sixteen years old. You stand about five foot _____ *(insert* **MARTHA**'s *height)* inches. And I'd put you in the neighborhood of, oh my... _____*(insert* **MARTHA**'s *weight)* ...give or take breakfast.

MARTHA. *(impressed)* Oh, my gosh, Mr. Primbody, how in the world do you know all that?

MR. PRIMBODY. It's a God-given gift. I used to deal in humanity. Wholesale. Until inflationary tendencies combined with an unsavory political climate to wash the bottom right out the tub. But I'm still a fair judge of flesh.

(The **CONDUCTOR** *passes through their car. He has a punch to process the ticket stubs.)*

CONDUCTOR. Tickets, please! Tickets! Cincinnati, Columbus, Wheeling, Washington, Baltimore, all points between!

(**PRIMBODY** *nudges* **DANTE**.)

MR. PRIMBODY. Dante? Dante? Dante – come to!

DANTE. *(slowly waking)* What, what, what, what?

MARTHA. Does this train go all the way to Philadelphia?

CONDUCTOR. You'll need to change locomotives in the Capitol, Miss.

(**DANTE** *sort of yawns, smacks his lips, and growls all at once, staring at* **MARTHA**.)

CONDUCTOR. Tickets, please.

MR. PRIMBODY. Isn't that a fine-how-do-you-do? It so happens that Dante and me are going to the Capitol, too.

MARTHA. Really?

MR. PRIMBODY. Ain't this a hoot?

DANTE. Mmmm, either I'm dreaming or you cut a right handsome figure of a lady.

MARTHA. How long does it take to get to Washington?

CONDUCTOR. Five days.

MR. PRIMBODY. Five days. You, me, and Dante. Like three Musketeers.

(*The* **CONDUCTOR** *exits, calling:*)

CONDUCTOR. Tickets, please, tickets!

(**PRIMBODY** *has pulled out a bottle of whiskey.*)

MR. PRIMBODY. Would you care for a sip, Miss?

MARTHA. No, thank you.

MR. PRIMBODY. It's good Kentucky bourbon. Smooth as the butt of a babe. Guaranteed.

MARTHA. Five days?

MR. PRIMBODY. Oh, time flies like a bird when you have pleasant company.

(sings:)

"I been drinking on the railroad – "

MR. PRIMBODY & DANTE. " – all the live long day!"

DANTE. *(softly, a rhythmic insert)* Boomba – boomba – boomba –

MR. PRIMBODY & DANTE. "I been drinking on the railroad, just to chug the time away!"

(Etc., as the train goes into a tunnel, overpowering their voices, as the lights fade a bit. The train whistle echos and becomes music...)

(Time, of course, passes...)

(A starry night on the railroad. **MARTHA** *has the flask now. She's more than a little "lit up" herself.)*

MR. PRIMBODY. To Henry Tall!

DANTE. Henry! God love him!

MARTHA. Oh, he has the bluest blue eyes and the winningest smile! I wish you all could meet. I know you'd both like him.

(She sighs, looks out the window.)

Ohhhhhh, lookit out there...! Look at those hills in the starlight. Have you ever seen anything so beautiful in all your life?

DANTE. Not with its clothes on.

*(***PRIMBODY*** hits **DANTE** with his hat.)*

MR. PRIMBODY. Knock it off, Dante, you stupid, ignorant wop. That's no way to talk to a lady.

DANTE. It ain't me, it's the liquor. Apologies, Miss.

MARTHA. Oh, I been around crass talk before.

(looks out the window again:)

I just can't get over how big this country is.

DANTE. Ohio's a fine state.

MR. PRIMBODY. This ain't Ohio, you ningkinpoop. Hell, we passed Wheeling an hour ago.

DANTE. Primbody and me once retrieved some, uh...contraband from just up outside Cincinnati. I was duly impressed with the land and her people. Good folk, the Buckeyes.

MARTHA. You two hunt down runaway slaves?

DANTE. On occasion. Uh huh.

MARTHA. But…you're a…Negro.

DANTE. *(a simple fact)* No, I'm not.

MARTHA. You're not?

MR. PRIMBODY. Dante's Eye-talian.

MARTHA. Eye-talian.

MR. PRIMBODY. A dark skinned, swarthy Eye-talian.

MARTHA. I'll be darn. I surely didn't mean no offense, Mr. Dante, it's just you're so dang…tan.

DANTE. Uh huh.

MARTHA. Henry says we ought to ship all the darkies back to Africa and give 'em their own country, but Willard, our house nigro – he's a real good butler – Willard says he don't want to go to Africa.

(in confidence)

I taught that big buck to read and write a little even though folks say that's liable to make him uppity. I'm just a freethinker, I reckon. I sorta reckon I might be a suffragist too. Pa says ladies got no place in politics – but this is one thing I really love about travelling – I never knew I had so dang many opinions, and then all a sudden I hear myself palavering with you two, and I think, good golly, well that ain't so dumb.

(They stare at her.)

I'm sorry. I'm hogging the bottle up, ain't I?

MR. PRIMBODY. No, no, you keep it, by all means.

DANTE. I've got to see a man about a horse, Miss. Excuse me.

MARTHA. What? Oh, I'm sorry. Go right ahead. Please.

*(***DANTE*** *exits.)*

MR. PRIMBODY. Man's got no more couth than a barnyard dog.

MARTHA. Can I tell you something? I know Dante's your friend and everything, but I don't appreciate the way he stares at me. Is it warm in here?

MR. PRIMBODY. Welp, I surely could do with a gulp of fresh air. Miss Martha, would you care to step out to the caboose with me?

MARTHA. I believe I would, Mister Primbody, thank you.

MR. PRIMBODY. Don't forget your handbag now.

(She stands, a little unsteady…)

Watch your step, Miss Martha. Even a wee sip of bourbon makes the world just a liiiiiittle bit wopper-jawed.

(They either exit and re-enter, or simply cross. Music informs the scene as the sky fills with stars. They are outdoors on the caboose. There's no need to change the set or add a rail or anything like that.)

MARTHA. Ohhhhhh! Dear Lord…! Look at all those stars! You know when Jonah was spit out from the belly of the beast and surrounded by darkness and water, he looked up at the sky, and said, "See the stars, how lofty they are. Is not God still in the height of heaven?"

MR. PRIMBODY. Is that Scripture, Miss Martha?

MARTHA. Oh, I can talk bible for miles, Mr. Primbody. Everyday, that's how we start the day back in Kentucky. Go ahead, choose a verse. Call out a chapter and turn me loose on it. I bet I can spit it right back at you.

*(**DANTE** walks up behind them, looking ominous in his long coat and derby style hat.)*

DANTE. Miss Martha. Primbody and me have hit on a long patch of mighty bad luck. So give us your purse and jump off the train.

MARTHA. You're pulling my leg.

*(**PRIMBODY** aims a rather imposing pistol at her.)*

MR. PRIMBODY. We never josh about robbery.

MARTHA. I can't jump. I'm pregnant. I might lose the baby.

MR. PRIMBODY. I'd hate to have to shoot you. You travel three or four days with somebody, they get to be family almost.

DANTE. A good Christian girl like you's packing a papoose?

MARTHA. You don't want to damn yourselves, do you? The bible makes no bones when it comes to killing.

DANTE. *(having second thoughts)* Maybe we ought to just tie her up, Percy.

MR. PRIMBODY. Now what kind of sense does that make?! What's gonna happen if somebody finds her out here all trussed up like a Christmas turkey, huh?? Honest to Christ, Dante, sometimes I don't know why I partner with you!

DANTE. Can't we at least take her a duds off and take turns with her?

MR. PRIMBODY. No! We're not playing hootchie-cootchie, you dumb shit ignorant greasy wop!

DANTE. Come on, Percy – just one quick poke! Don't you wanta peek at them titties?

MR. PRIMBODY. *(considers)* Well. OK. But I poke first.

(**MARTHA** *hits* **PRIMBODY** *over the head with the whiskey bottle. It breaks; his knees buckle. She grabs his pistol, and brandishes it at* **DANTE.**)

DANTE. This whole scheme was his idea, see? Primbody's bad to the core! I tried to talk him out of it, but I ain't got no say-so with Primbody. Please, God, don't yank the trigger.

MARTHA. You ain't fit to walk the earth, Dante.

DANTE. You're not gonna shoot me. You wouldn't know how.

(*She shoots him. BOOM! The shot echoes like doom itself.* **DANTE** *falls.*)

(**MARTHA** *looks up at the heavens in the flickering, fading light:*)

MARTHA. Nobody's going to heaven now.

(*Thunder/cannon sound. The* **MEN** *strike the "train" chairs as the track sounds turn into weird telegraphic tapping.*)

(*Tight light on* **HENRY** *in a proper blue Union uniform. He faces downstage. He is somehow formal and vulnerable in the same breath.*)

HENRY. "My dearest Martha. Stop. I don't rightly know if this wire will find you or not. Stop. I send you this message as a matter of honor because I have met somebody else. Stop. I met another person I'm sweet on. Stop. I hope you do not despise me. Stop. I hope that we can still be good…pals, like before. Stop. Our regiment is bivouacked ten miles outside Washington, but so far I have not seen a single Rebel. Stop. I hope that will change real soon. Stop. My deepest respects to you and the Reverend. Stop. Your friend from home, Henry Tall. Stop."

(Thunder. Lightening. An eerie, eerie wind.)

(Lights rise on MR. PRIMBODY *in the storm.* PRIMBODY*'s head is wrapped in a bloody bandage. He turns his face heavenward:)*

MR. PRIMBODY. Rain!! Rain!! Go ahead, spit on me! Drown me! Wash me away! I don't care! What do I have to live for? Treat me like a bug you big fat bastard clouds! Rain on me! Rain!

(Lightning and thunder. MARTHA *enters dressed in Dante's long coat and derby hat with her hair tucked up under. She looks a lot like a man.)*

MR. PRIMBODY. *(cont.)* Here I am! Go ahead! Strike me down, Jesus! Come on! I darest you! Don't be a pussy!

MARTHA. Mister Primbody, quit taking the lord's name in vain. I know we're in a pickle, but –

MR. PRIMBODY. A pickle? A pickle?? I loved that swarthy Eye-talian like a brother and now he is dead. That's not a pickle – that's emptiness. Loneliness. Solitude.

(then)

Good God, you look so much like him in that get-up, I'd just like to haul off and hug you close to me.

MARTHA. I'm in this disguise cause the law's on my tail, not to tickle your fancy.

MR. PRIMBODY. Emptiness! Loneliness! Solitude! I never had any family. No younguns. Nobody but Dante. It sorta warms up my insides to call you my own.

MARTHA. If I can just get to D.C. and go to the War Department, surely they'll know where Henry is. That's a good plan, don't you think?

MR. PRIMBODY. You'll need to bribe 'em. And last time I checked Dante's pockets, he was clean outa coinage.

(**MARTHA** *might try to hand him the pistol, which is in* **DANTE**'s *coat pocket.*)

MARTHA. Then go rob somebody.

MR. PRIMBODY. I don't have the constitution for it. Not no more. After Dante bought a one-way ticket to the pearly gates and I woke up with my head bashed in, I promised my maker I'd change my stripes, boy. From this time forth I'm giving up back-stabbing, stealing, cheating, whiskey, card tricks, and sex outsides the bonds of matrimony.

(*Thunder cracks.*)

Excepting in cases of exceptional need, of course. Yessir! I feel as if God has looked down upon me and given me a chance at screwing my life up all over again. Tragedy has made of me a better individual. That Roman did not die in vain!

(*A bell rings, like a church bell crossed with a cow bell. It rings three times. Lights change. The rain has stopped. rays of sunlight shine through the clouds. The sky is blood-red with wispy clouds in it.*)

(*We hear a cow bell off-stage. A threadbare refugee* **FARMER** *enters, with a rope in his hand, that stretches off-stage. The* **FARMER** *says from the depths of his soul:*)

FARMER. Repent. Repent.

COW. (*offstage*) Moo. Moo.

FARMER. Repent.

(*His* **COW** *enters with a frayed old rope around its neck. The* **COW** *is played by the same actor who played* **DANTE**. *He's dressed in tattered clothes, bare-footed, with a cow bell around his neck, and white make-up around* *one eye. Nothing else is needed to tell us who he is. Note: the* **COW** *should be played as a pure and simple, long-suffering cow, without any hint of attitude.)*

*(***MR. PRIMBODY*** *is immediately taken with the bovine, and can't keep his eyes off of it.)*

COW. Moo.

FARMER. Repent.

MARTHA. Could I possibly beg some milk from you?

FARMER. Repent I say.

MARTHA. I could repent a lot faster with food on my stomach.

FARMER. You Yankees or Rebels?

MR. PRIMBODY. Which side are you on?

FARMER. This war is evil. I'm taking my worldly possessions and leaving this country.

COW. Moo. Moo.

MARTHA. Where you gonna go?

FARMER. I'm gonna keep hiking straight down this highway until I find God, and when I do, I'm gonna give Him an earful. I never seen so much evil as waits up the road. Turn around. Head the other direction, boys. Run! There's terrible fighting up there.

MR. PRIMBODY. That sure is a fine looking bovine.

FARMER. I'd give you some milk, but I don't have a bucket.

MR. PRIMBODY. That's mighty white of you.

MARTHA. We been traipsing for days without sight of nothing but burned down houses and fields picked bare as the heart of a sinner.

COW. Moo.

FARMER. The end of the world is at hand.

COW. Moo.

MR. PRIMBODY. Hey, Farmer? Wait up.

MARTHA. Mister Primbody?

MR. PRIMBODY. I got a notion to traipse up the Jesus Road with him.

MARTHA. But what about me?

FARMER. Confess your sins, pilgrim, and come along with us.

MARTHA. I can't. I've gotta find Henry. I know he'll want to do the right thing by me.

MR. PRIMBODY. Oh, Christ on crutch – you don't even know which side he's a fighting fer.

MARTHA. He's for the Union. I think. 'Cept that don't make sense since Kentucky's a slave state and sorta for the South.

MR. PRIMBODY. Kentucky's confused.

FARMER. Repent I say.

COW. Moo.

FARMER. I say turn your tail to evil and run.

COW. Moo. Moo.

> *(The* **FARMER** *and his* **COW** *start off.)*

MR. PRIMBODY. I'm gonna follow that cow clean to God. Good bye, son. Good luck with the baby.

FARMER. Repent.

COW. Moo.

MR. PRIMBODY. *(trying the word on for size)* Repent!

COW. *(not so great)* Moo.

MR. PRIMBODY. Repent!

COW. *(better…)* Moo.

FARMER. For the reckoning time is at hand.

COW. Moo.

MR. PRIMBODY. Repent!

COW. Moo.

MR. PRIMBODY. *(exiting)* Repent! Repent!

COW. Moo. Moo.

> *(***MARTHA** *is all alone. A bell rings four times, and with each ring the stage changes in definite beats. One ring: blackout. Two rings: instant stars. Three rings: side light. Four rings: tight light on* **MARTHA**'s *face only,*

all the other lights are gone. Dante's derby hat is off. Her hair looks a little wild. She talks without a great deal of outward emotion. Standing upright...somewhat detached, as if reporting/recalling:)

MARTHA. *(to the theatre)* I am asleep now. I dream of my mother. I am told that she died giving birth to my life. And I am afraid that the cry of newborn will herald my death, and the same thing will happen to me.

(then)

In my dream I am in a large house. I look for my mother. I open a closet. A body falls from it. I study it closely. I feel the flesh of its hand in my own. This is not my mother. This is a child with hair like my own. I see welts rising like the stripes of a flag on her back where her father's belt meted out discipline. This child is marked by the gospel. John 14:6. I am the way and the truth and the light, saith the Lord. And no one shall come to the father, except by me. Blood. Water. Trees. Grass. Houses. Colors. Blue. Yellow. Purple. Red. All these things live in my dream. I do not understand them. And when I awake, I forget these things. Now.

(Thunder and cannons echo, lights flicker as the screaming whistle of the bombardment brings us to a battlefield encampment. The shelling continues, not constant but methodical, as:)

*(Lights rise on **TWO UNION SOLDIERS**. **SOLDIER #2** is played by a black man in white face – the same actor who played Willard, Dante, and the Cow. It is winter. It's cold. The **SOLDIERS** are sorely afraid. Snow is falling, or the image of snow falling is projected on the upstage wall. Note: nothing is needed to tell us where we are except for the soldiers, the sound-scape, the lights, and good acting.)*

SOLDIER #1. I thought you said the durn Rebs never shelled us at night. I thought you swore they were low on supplies and out of ammunition.

SOLDIER #2. Aw, they just want to dog us, that's all. Keep us awake at night. Keep us off balance.

SOLDIER #1. I never thought I'd say this, but I miss Fort Wayne.

(Another whistling shell explodes. **SOLDIER #2** *has a metal box of matches.)*

My damned ear drums're like to explode. Jesus, Jeb, what are you doing?

SOLDIER #2. I'm freezing. I'm starting a fire.

(A campfire glows – either shining up from a trap, or lit from above. They crouch close and warm their hands.)

SOLDIER #1. I heard the dangdest durn thing in the world today.

SOLDIER #2. What's that?

SOLDIER #1. The Quartermaster told me that somebody told him that old Uncle Abe took complete leave of his senses.

SOLDIER #2. Abe Lincoln?

SOLDIER #1. He told me Abe went plumb crazy and freed all the niggers.

SOLDIER #2. When?

SOLDIER #1. Yesterday. New Years. Said just like that, he proclaimed 'em free. Now you're slaves. Now you ain't. Poof. Free.

SOLDIER #2. Aw, that's just one of those addle-brained rumors the Rebs like to spread. Lincoln'd never do something as dumb as that.

SOLDIER #1. Jeb, I don't mind a fair and square fight, and I'm all for saving the Union, whatever that means – but I'm not gonna get my butt shot at for no pickaninnies. If it comes to that – Fort Wayne, I'm home.

*(***MARTHA*** enters, dressed in a standard issue blue Union uniform. Her clothes cover her growing pregnancy. She doesn't lower her voice to play a "man," she just changes her attitude a little.* **MARTHA/MARTIN** *is holding a half-eaten corn cob.)*

Hey, Martin.

MARTHA/MARTIN. Hey, fellas.

SOLDIER #2. Martin, you eat more than any damn soldier I ever saw.

(She crosses to their fire.)

SOLDIER #1. What're you gnawing on now?

MARTHA/MARTIN. Corn cob.

SOLDIER #2. Are you putting weight on?

MARTHA/MARTIN. I don't know. Why? You want to make something of it?

SOLDIER #2. No. No.

SOLDIER #1. The rest of the boys just get reedier, littler all the time, Martin, but you just get fatter. Can you explain to me why that is?

MARTHA/MARTIN. Nope.

(MARTHA/MARTIN takes a bite of corn as another Union Man enters. SERGEANT MCMURPHY is died-in-the-wool Irish, with a brogue, and an effortless sense of authority.)

SOLDIER #1. Hey, Sarge. What's doing?

MCMURPHY. We're under strict orders tonight for no campfires, lads. Straight from the General himself. McClellan might have the bloody "slows", but he doesn't intend to give our position away.

SOLDIER #2. But it's cold, Sergeant.

MCMURPHY. Ladies, we're just born to suffer. That's all there is to it.

SOLDIER #1. Well, shit.

SOLDIER #2. I'll stamp it out.

SOLDIER #1. Don't stamp on it. Piss on it.

(The two SOLDIERS turn their backs to us to "piss out" the fire. MARTHA/MARTIN continues to gnaw at his/her food.)

SOLDIER #2. Hey, Martin?

MARTHA/MARTIN. Yeah?

SOLDIER #2. Don't you want to piss on it?

MARTHA/MARTIN. Not now. I'm eating.

SOLDIER #1. *(over his shoulder)* I heard somebody robbed the supply tent last night.

MCMURPHY. You don't say?

SOLDIER #1. *(pulling his fly up)* Pilfered a side of cured bacon, yep. That's what I heard.

MCMURPHY. You wouldn't happen to know something about that now, Martin?

MARTHA/MARTIN. If I knew who took it, I'd find him and eat it.

SOLDIER #2. I believe you would, Martin. I believe you would.

MCMURPHY. Martin, my boy, you're on picket duty tonight. The rest of you lads better hit the hay.

(Fog begins rolling in. A whistling shell falls in the distance.)

SOLDIER #1. I can't sleep when they're shelling like this.

MCMURPHY. Word has it there'll be some hard fighting come morn. Rest while you can, lads. Sleep while you're able.

SOLDIER #2. Good night, Sarge.

SOLDIER #1. Night, Martin.

MARTHA/MARTIN. Good night, fellahs.

SOLDIER #1. Night, Sarge.

*(**SOLDIERS** exit. Whistling shells falling closer now.)*

MCMURPHY. Sweet dreams to you, lads. Keep your eyes open, Martin, and God save the Union…whatever that means.

*(**MCMURPHY** exits. **MARTHA/MARTIN** is alone on stage with her rifle. A shell falls much closer. Explosion. Lights are changing. Sounds of ominous buzzing and music, like haywire crickets. More fog. Rebel yells. Battle sounds. Horses. Possible projections of Civil War battlefield photographs as Martha sinks to her knees, and covers her ears. War sounds/music build to a distinct crescendo… then:)*

(Immediate tight light on **MARTHA**. *All sounds disappear except for music.)*

MARTHA. Bodies. Bodies everywhere around me. I can't find the earth for the bodies upon it. I am crawling on bodies; running atop of bodies. Blood soaks the ground. I run and I run. I trip and I fall and I think for a moment I've died. I feel myself rising like a bird above the fields of battle, and everywhere I can see blood. The landscape is nothing but bodies and more bodies piled like stove wood clean up to the heavens. I fly past the hospital tent. Arms and legs sawn clean and tossed off like kindling. More arms and legs have littered the earth now than stars in the sky, and still, I continue to fly. I can't feel my legs. I can't find enough breath to sustain me. I think that I hear myself screaming. Crying. I feel my baby. Kicking. And turning. I feel it gripping my heart with its fist, and I know that it wants to be born! I can't have a baby in a world like this!

(then)

My blood is its air now; my womb is its earth. I have a planet that spins in my body. A planet with perfect little fingers and toes and cheeks twice as soft as a warm autumn rain. I close my eyes and I feel the universe calming within me. I breathe. And I pray. And finally, finally...the contractions stop.

(The sound of a screeching hawk. Lights change.)

(A **ONE-LEGGED OFFICER** *enters on crutches. A uniformed soldier is nearby.)*

ONE-LEGGED OFFICER. Where the hell do you think you're running to, boy?

MARTHA/MARTIN. I want to go home.

ONE-LEGGED OFFICER. Get back to your outfit.

MARTHA/MARTIN. No.

ONE-LEGGED OFFICER. Look, son, I'm not gonna tell you again. Now get the hell back to the fight.

MARTHA/MARTIN. I don't care what happens. I'm not going back.

ONE-LEGGED OFFICER. Boy, do you know what they do to deserters? They hang 'em by the neck, and leave em to rot to rancid meat in the sun. Is that what you want?

MARTHA/MARTIN. I don't care.

ONE-LEGGED OFFICER. Corporal, get over here.

GUARD. Yes, sir?

ONE-LEGGED OFFICER. Place this boy under arrest.

GUARD. Yes, sir.

ONE-LEGGED OFFICER. What's your name, boy?

MARTHA/MARTIN. I don't know.

ONE-LEGGED OFFICER. Tell me your name.

MARTHA/MARTIN. I don't know.

ONE-LEGGED OFFICER. Hang him in the morning.

GUARD. Yes, sir.

 *(The **ONE-LEGGED OFFICER** exits. The **GUARD** places manacles on **MARTHA/MARTIN**.)*

 *(Sound of chains. Lights rise on the stockade. **TWO UNION SOLDIERS** are in leg irons. **HENRY** and **LANFORD**, who happens to be a black man.)*

HENRY. *(moaning)* Water…water…

LANFORD. Please…we need water.

GUARD. Aw, quit your damn bellering, would you?

 *(meaning **MARTHA**)*

 I got some fresh meat for you, boys.

LANFORD. Water, please.

GUARD. I thought I told you to shut the hell up. You're all gonna hang first thing in the morning. I bet you'll live through the night without a little sip of wa-wa to go sleepy by. You yellow-bellied, nigger-loving turncoats.

 *(The **GUARD** kicks **LANFORD**, and then exits.)*

LANFORD. Ahh!

HENRY. Oh, Lord love a goose.

MARTHA. *(realizing, as if in a dream)* Henry?

HENRY. Lanford, are you alright?

MARTHA. Henry, is that you?

HENRY. Who the hell are you, Mister?

MARTHA. You're Henry Tall. Henry, from Look Out, Kentucky.

LANFORD. Hey, buddy, get your hands off him.

MARTHA. Henry, it's me, Henry. Martha! It's me! I can't believe I found you! What are you doing down here?

HENRY. I'm a prisoner, Martha. How in God's name did you? – What are you doing all dressed up like? – Lord love a goose, Martha! Look at you!

LANFORD. Martha, are you a girl?

HENRY. Lanford, I'd like you to meet, Martha. Martha, this is Lanford. The best friend I ever made.

MARTHA. Henry, why are they hanging you?

HENRY. I turned tail and run, Martha. I don't have the first ounce of bravery in me.

LANFORD. There's all kinds of bravery, Henry. You're brave in other ways.

HENRY. Thank you, Lanford.

MARTHA. Henry, I got some big news for you.

HENRY. Martha, did you get my wire?

MARTHA. Did you get my letters? I wrote you a million times over.

HENRY. No, I sure didn't.

MARTHA. Henry: I'm having a baby. Your baby. Our baby. We're having a youngster. And I mean I'm gonna be having it soon. You remember that time by the river that night? You told me you cared for me, Henry – remember? Well, that night is about bear fruit in a real big way.

HENRY. Martha?

MARTHA. I feel like I got my voice back. Like I've been locked in this mute kind of cage for so long without you to talk to.

HENRY. Martha?

MARTHA. Oh, Henry, I'm so glad I've found you. Tell me everything's gonna be alright. Even if we die in the morning, just tell me you love me.

HENRY. I'm already took, Martha.

MARTHA. What do you mean?

HENRY. I fibbed to you, Martha. I'm not in the stockade for running from Rebels. I got put here for telling the truth as I see it.

MARTHA. What do you mean?

HENRY. I mean that Lanford and me are kind of a couple.

MARTHA. A couple what, Henry?

LANFORD. Martha, we're two individuals in love.

(**HENRY** *takes* **LANFORD**'s *hand. Note: neither* **HENRY** *or* **LANFORD** *is "fey" in the least.*)

HENRY. I told my Captain about us; he didn't take the news too well at all. But Lanford has taught me that people are people. No matter what sort and what color. Do you know that he went to Harvard? That ought to give you some indication of how smart he is. The very first freed-man to graduate, Martha. He went to the same school your pa did. I tell you, sometimes the world is too small.

LANFORD. Love is a transcendent thing, Martha.

HENRY. But most folks don't see it that way.

(**MARTHA** *stares at them.*)

MARTHA. *(to the theatre)* I can't wait to hang.

(*Blackout. A bell rings four times − like a church bell. Wind blows. Night birds call to each other, and this sound is something like music.* **LANFORD** *speaks to the theatre, lit by a special:*)

LANFORD. Martha is asleep now. So I will speak for her. She dreams about Henry. She thinks: I wrote poems for that boy. She thinks: I did his homework. She thinks,

I agreed with him even when he said stupid things. I took all my clothes off. I gave him my body. I left home to find him. I murdered to find him. And he is in love with another. My baby's father is in love with a man. Who is black. And all of us are destined to die.

(Lights rise…the shadows of bars crisscross the floor. We are in the stockade at night. In the dim light we see that **HENRY** *is wearing a dress over his uniform.)*

MARTHA. Henry? Can I ask you something? Why are you wearing a dress?

HENRY. Because it's yours. Because I found it in your knapsack while you cried in your sleep. Because you wore it on the night we made love. I wanted to touch you, but I was afraid you might waken. So I held it to my cheek…and then it was on me.

MARTHA. Henry, you do me love, don't you?! Oh, God, I knew so. I felt it was true.

HENRY. This material is so soft.

MARTHA. It's calico.

HENRY. It's just the best stuff I ever felt.

LANFORD. Henry?

HENRY. Yes, Lanford?

LANFORD. I have a plan to escape. Martha, you need to pretend you're a girl.

MARTHA. Lanford –

HENRY. I love this plan.

MARTHA. You haven't even heard it yet.

LANFORD. I want you to scream like a helpless female until the guard hears you.

HENRY. I love this plan.

LANFORD. He won't expect to find a woman in the stockade –

HENRY. – And I can pretend that I'm you! Is that right? Is that the plan, Lanford? I knew it. I told you he's smart.

LANFORD. While you use your womanly wiles to distract the guard, Henry and I will subdue him.

HENRY. Because he'll think I'm you! It's a brilliant plan, Lanford.

MARTHA. If he thinks you're me, then what good is me using my wiles gonna do?

HENRY. If anyone's going to be taken undue advantage of, Martha, I'd rather it be me than you. Society may brand me a pervert for liking Lanford and sharing the love which dare not speak its name, but I want our kid to grow up in a better world. I don't think that's too much to ask. I want a world where justice and-and-and freedom, and dare I say chivalry? –

LANFORD. Sure.

HENRY. – where these things are more than ineffectual noises men make while they wave swords at each other because politicians told them to. Be he a boy or be he a girl, I want our kid to be proud of his Pa. And if I have to wear a dress to accomplish that, Martha, then, by God, just pass out the bonnets.

(**HENRY** *puts a bonnet on.*)

(**MARTHA** *looks at* **HENRY** *and screams.*)

GUARD. *(offstage)* Hey, pipe down down there!

(*The* **GUARD** *enters jangling his big ring of keys.*)

What the sam hill's going on down here? Huh? What is that ruckus? Who is that?

(**MARTHA** *takes her Union soldier's cap off.*)

MARTHA. Me, sir.

(*The* **GUARD** *takes a closer look at* **MARTHA**.)

GUARD. Good lord…you're a girl. You know the rules, missy. No whores allowed in the stockade, gosh durnit. They'll have my stripes for this.

(**HENRY** *steps forward in his bonnet. He does not act like a "girl" in the least; if anything, his dress and bonnet have made him into more of a chivalrous man.*)

HENRY. Unhand her this instant. If you have a bone to pick, pick it with me.

GUARD. How many painted ladies are in here? This ain't a stockade, it's a house of ill repute. Who'dja bribe? How'd you hussies get in here?

HENRY. Um. We came in the night.

GUARD. Oh, I bet you did. I got a mighty, mighty sociable friend in my trousers. Why don't you drop to your knees and strike up a quick conversation?

*(**HENRY** reluctantly kneels in front of the **GUARD**. **LANFORD** creeps up behind the **GUARD**. Wraps a chain around his neck, and starts to strangle him.)*

Mercy!

LANFORD. Keys, Henry. Take his gun, Martha.

(They gets the keys and the gun.)

MARTHA. Don't kill him.

LANFORD. Why not?

MARTHA. 'Cause I've seen enough killing, that's why.

*(**LANFORD** stops choking the **GUARD**, who sinks to his knees, coughing and gasping. As they unlock their irons, the **GUARD** wraps his arms around **MARTHA**'s legs.)*

GUARD. Bless you, boy. Bless you. Tu clementiam invetius semper habem!

HENRY. Good lord, he's talking in tongues.

LANFORD. That's not the Holy Ghost, Henry, it's Latin.

GUARD. My name is Horace Eugenie. I used to teach sweet, little, soap-smelling, apple-cheeked younguns in a white one-room school house in Lima, Ohio, which though, sadly, not the home of the lima bean is my hearth and home. Ask anybody who hails from Lima. I'm a kind person. But this war has turned my heart into an ugly, little walnut. Bless you, boy. Thank you for saving my bacon.

(He proclaims:)

Tu clementiam inventius semper habem!

MARTHA. What in tarnation does that even mean?

GUARD. May You Live As Long As Life Is Worth Living!

LANFORD. Martha, let's go.

HENRY. The sun's almost up. We better make tracks before they come to hang us.

(*As they exit, the* **GUARD** *proclaims in a language of his own twisted invention:*)

GUARD. Tu clementiam inventius semper habem!

(*Music changes. Lights change.*)

(*A bright shaft of light shines down on* **MARTHA,** **LANFORD,** *and* **HENRY** *in his dress and bonnet. Flower petals don't drift from the heavens, but it feels like they could.*)

LANFORD. Free at last! Freedom at last! Thank the Transcendental Power, we are free at last!

HENRY. Where to now, Lanford?

LANFORD. West, Henry. Westward to wilderness, fecundity, and fields as lush as the dreams of a farm boy.

HENRY. (*looking downstage*) There's a whole lotta country out there.

LANFORD. If we push far enough West, we'll come to country where there is no more country. Then we can found our own country.

HENRY. We'll find it and found it.

(**HENRY** *and* **LANFORD** *are about to kiss.*)

MARTHA. Okay. Look, fellahs, I just want a safe place to have my little baby.

HENRY. Our baby, Martha. Yours, mine, and Lanford's. We're like two Josephs and a Mary.

MARTHA. I can't set up housekeeping with two husbands, Henry, especially when my husbands only want to have, you know, relations with each other.

HENRY. Once we start our own country, them kinda things won't matter a'tall. You can have as many husbands as you feel like having.

LANFORD. Yes sir, we're freedom bound now!

(*Whereupon, a tattered, barefoot* **SLAVE** *enters. He is a white man in black face. He carries the body of his master on his back. His master is a life-sized dummy dressed in a Rebel Colonel's uniform with a bloody bandage around his head. Blood from the dummy forms a huge stain on the* **SLAVE**'*s threadbare back.*)

LANFORD. Hold on a second, brother. Who's that you're lugging around on your back?

SLAVE. My Master. Da Colonel. He's been gutshot. I gots to carry him home, to da home-place – to mistress and chil'en and chittlens and cotton!

LANFORD. You've been emancipated, friend. Our people are free now. You don't have to do this.

SLAVE. Let me tell you something, boy. I'm a happy slave. Personally, I find it's a privilege to be owned by some-body. Now dat is commitment, boy. Dat humbles marriage. I'm his for life. Are you free?

LANFORD. Yes.

SLAVE. I feel sorry for you. I don't needs to fret about nothing. Food, shelter, love – I don't fret it. When it's slave-making time, da Master, he picks out a woman, we breed, and dat's dat. I'm happy to serve him. I'm free in ways you can't even imagine.

LANFORD. What's your name?

SLAVE. Frank White.

LANFORD. Frank, I think you've got some issues.

SLAVE. You wasting my time.

(*The* **SLAVE** *starts to exit.*)

HENRY. Frank?

SLAVE. (*turns on a dime*) Yes, Ma'am...Mister Boss...person.

HENRY. Frank, Lanford and I are in love. Now I'm white and he's black, but we see beyond race and gender. So why don't heave ho that burden and come along with us? We're heading out West, Frank, to start a new country.

VE. What'ch'all think I am – stupid? I gots to get da Colonel back to da home-place.

MARTHA. The Colonel's dead, Frank.

SLAVE. What do you mean?

MARTHA. I mean he's done bled clean to death. All over you, looks like.

(*The* **SLAVE** *turns in a circle, trying to see the man on his back.*)

SLAVE. He's dead?

LANFORD. Um-hum.

SLAVE. *(wary)* You sure about dat?

MARTHA. Um-hum.

(*The* **SLAVE** *looks at her hard. Then puts the Colonel dummy down.*)

SLAVE. Let me just see if his ticker's still beating.

(*He puts his ear the Colonel's heart.*)

SLAVE. Aw, lawrd. Lawdy, lawdy, lawdy.

(*The* **SLAVE** *makes a sound that's something like a moan and a mournful scream mixed together. Then he pulls out a knife and stabs his master's heart.*)

MARTHA. Frank, for pity's sake.

(*The* **SLAVE** *stabs the dummy again and again. He rips its guts open and starts yanking feathers and stuffing and red ribbons from its insides. He absolutely desecrates the body. Furious, frantic, as if in a fit. Feathers drift through the air. He cuts its arms and legs off.*)

HENRY. I can totally identify with that feeling.

SLAVE. *(stops, turns, level)* Don't you presume to know how I feel. You don't have a clue about me.

(*The* **SLAVE** *goes back to wailing away at the dummy.*)

HENRY. Frank, I know the whole slavery thing was no picnic. I get that. I do. But you've got a find a healthier place to put all this anger. Otherwise, it's gonna destroy you.

(The SLAVE stares at him, holding a severed limb.)

Now why don't you close your eyes and visualize a happier time and place? Can you try that with me? Let's visualize the future together.

(HENRY has his hand on the SLAVE's shoulder. The SLAVE plunges the knife into HENRY.)

SLAVE. *(level)* Visualize dat.

HENRY. Lord love a goose.

MARTHA. Frank, what have you done?

(LANFORD cradles the dying HENRY in his arms.)

LANFORD. Oh, my God. Oh, my God, Henry. How did this happen? Why did this happen?

MARTHA. Frank, he was trying to help you!

SLAVE. Oh, lawdy, I done stabbed a white woman.

LANFORD. This man is no woman! This man is my life! Lord, Frank, and here I felt kinship with you!

SLAVE. I ain't gonna swing from no tree for no Uncle Tom's whitey.

(The SLAVE exits.)

MARTHA. Don't die, Henry. Please, keep your eyes open.

HENRY. *(weak)* Lanford...?

LANFORD. I'm not gonna leave you.

MARTHA. Oh, God – oh, Jesus, how can we help him? Lanford, I can't lose the love of my life. I can't lose my baby's father. Please. Please. We have to save him.

(Music. HENRY has died. After a moment...)

LANFORD. He's transcended, Martha. His soul's in the place we've been taught to call heaven.

(MARTHA backs away. Looks at the BLOOD on her hands.)

MARTHA. I can't have a baby in a country like this.

(LANFORD stays with HENRY.)

LANFORD. Listen to me: the soul is transformative, Martha. We despair and we grieve, but we have to believe that it all has a purpose.

MARTHA. What purpose, Lanford? Death and destruction? Madness and mayhem?

LANFORD. Martha: you carry his child. His soul lives in you.

MARTHA. I'm not birthing it.

LANFORD. You're too far along to get rid of it now.

MARTHA. I've stopped my contractions before; I'll stop em again.

LANFORD. You can't stop the wheel of life and death, Martha.

MARTHA. Don't you understand?! I've carried this kid through the mud and the blood from Fort Sumter to Sharpsburg. I've been pregnant for almost three years.

LANFORD. Three years.

MARTHA. *(a declaration to the heavens, the world, and the theatre)* I swear to God I'm not birthing my baby til I find a better world than this.

(Music cresendos…)

(Lights to black. Curtain.)

End of Act One

ACT TWO: A BETTER WORLD

(Wind blows. Night birds call to each other. A bell rings four times – a perfect, clarion sound.)

(Lights rise on **MARTHA***. If the theatre has an American flag curtain, then she stands before it. She is very pregnant. She is wearing the blood-stained dress that* **HENRY** *was killed in. It has bloody handprints on the belly. She wears her Union Army jacket over it.)*

MARTHA. *(She speaks to the theatre:)* It is the best of dreams. It is the worst of dreams. I am alone in a house with many rooms. A door opens. I see a child with hair like my own. I have not met my mother before, but I know now this child is her.

(Music sneaks in, transforming the wind, supporting her thoughts.)

I feel a hand on my waist. We turn, and we spin, and walls and floors and doors fall away. The ceiling is sky now. The earth but a shadow. And the eyes of my mother are shining like two perfect moons. I throw back my head and I breathe in the taste and texture of her breath as if I am bathing myself in the warmest of waters. And she grows. My mother grows, larger and larger. Until she stands taller than ten thousand steeples. She picks me up; like a tiny, little lady bug perched on the cusp of her pinkish white fingers. This child. This giant. This mother whose face I have never seen, holds me in her palm and she dances! With me! I do not understand why I dream of this. But when I awake, I vow from my soul I will never forget this sensation. For this is the love which a mother can bear for her child. And I shall remember this. Now.

Lights rise on a starry, Union blue sky. Two moons are in the sky, like two yellow eyes. We are on the great prairie.)

(MOTHER COW and her CALF stand in the grass. They are fairly cow-like in behavior at first. MOTHER COW is dressed in a brown and white, cow-patterned prairie-style skirt, a brown blouse, and a cow-patterned bonnet. Her CALF is dressed in cow-patterned over-alls. They both have cow bells around their necks. They are both barefoot.)

MOTHER COW. Moo. Moo.

CALF. Moo. Moo. Moo. Moo.

MOTHER COW. Moo. Moo.

MARTHA. Tell me something, Mother Milk Cow – am I seeing double tonight, or are there two yellow moons shining bright over the great western prairie?

MOTHER COW. Moon. Moon.

MARTHA. That's just what I thought. There *are* two moons.

CALF. Moon. Moon.

MARTHA. Mother Cow, would you mind if asked you a personal question?

MOTHER COW. Moo.

MARTHA. Did it hurt when you birthed your calf? I bet it did, huh?

MOTHER COW. *(it hurt like heck)* Moo.

MARTHA. You know my mother bled to death when she labored with me.

MOTHER COW. *(sad)* Moo. Moo.

CALF. *(plaintive)* Mooooo. Mooooo.

MARTHA. It's a strange kinda thing how much you can pine for somebody you never even knew.

MOTHER COW. Moo.

MARTHA. I don't want that to happen to my little angel.

CALF. Moo.

MOTHER COW. Moo.

(**MARTHA** *says simply, and from the depths of her*

MARTHA. Moo.

(*The* **COWS** *feel her loss…*)

MOTHER COW. Moo.

CALF. Moo.

MARTHA. Moo.

MOTHER COW. Moo.

CALF. Moo.

MARTHA. Moo.

MOTHER COW. Moo.

MARTHA. Moo.

CALF. Moo.

MOTHER COW. Moo.

MARTHA. Moo? Moo?

MOTHER COW. Moo, moo, moo.

(*Gradually the grieving, plaintive moos begin to change to moos of concern and communion.*)

CALF. Moo.

MOTHER COW. Moo.

MARTHA. Moo, moo, moo, moo!

MOTHER COW. Moo!

CALF. Moo-moo-moo-moo – moo!

MOTHER COW. Moo, moo.

(*The* **COWS** *nuzzle* **MARTHA** *and they all three moo softly together for a moment…then:*)

MARTHA. I know, I know, Mother Milk Cow, you're absolutely right. I *do* need to look on the bright side. I don't know what I've been such a big scaredy cat for.

MOTHER COW. Moo.

MARTHA. People been birthing babies forever like falling off a log. How hard can it be?

CALF. Moo!

'Cepting I don't want to bleed clean to death; s, I don't have a husband, or money or any idea ow to raise a youngster since'n I basically raised up my motherless myself and I turned out to be a hermit who's crazy as a bed bug and talks to her stupid ole bovines all day.

COWS. *(their feelings are hurt)* Moo. Moo.

MARTHA. Oh, now, don't you be petulant. Don't take that tone with me, Milk Cows. You know I didn't mean no offense.

COWS. *(maybe, maybe not)* Moo. Moo.

(To make them feel better, **MARTHA** *sings a little song acapella.)*

MARTHA.
OHHHHHHH, I LOVE MY BOVINES, AND MY BOVINES LOVE ME.

COWS. *(sing, tentative at first)*
MOO.

MARTHA.
WE LIKE TO GRAZE ON THE OPEN PRAIRIE.

COWS.
MOO.

MARTHA.
WE SING A MOURNFUL SONG, AND WE CROON A MOURNFUL TOOOOOON.

COWS. *(rising scale)*
MOO MOO MOO MOO MOOOOOOOOON!

MARTHA.
OHHHH, I LOVE MY BOVS CAUSE MY BOVS LOVE TO MOO!

(Music sneaks in as this turns into a Western-style oom-pa-pa:)

COWS.
MOO, MOO-MOO. MOO, MOO-MOO. MOO, MOO-MOO. MOO, MOO-MOO.

MARTHA.

COWS DON'T PASS JUDGEMENT –

COWS.

MOO.

MARTHA.

– COWS JUST PASS GAS.

COWS.

WE DON'T FRET THE FUTURE OR DWELL ON THE PAST.

MARTHA.

IF YOU'RE IN DESPAIR FOR THE GREAT HERE AND NOW
LOOK ON THE BRIGHT SIDE.....

COWS & MARTHA.

.....AND MOURN WITH A COW!
COWS DON'T PASS JUDGEMENT (MOO),
COWS JUST PASS GAS
COWS DON'T FRET THE FUTURE OR DWELL ON THE PAST.

COWS.

OH, SHE DON'T MISS CIVILIZATION AT ALL!

MARTHA. (*big sustained phrase*)

THE ONLY THING I MISS IS DEAD HENRY TALL!

(**LANFORD** *enters during the interlude. He's dressed in a brown suit, circa 1890, with a starched collar and a bowler hat. He has a small, worn out old suitcase. He's a little stooped, a lot older than he used to be.*)

COWS & MARTHA.

MOO, ONE-TWO
MOO, THREE-FOUR
MOO MOO MOO MOOOOOOOOO
MOO, ONE-TWO
MOO, THREE-FOUR
MOO MOO MOO MOOOOOOOOO
MOO, MOO-MOO
MOO, MOO-MOO
MOO MOO MOO MOOOOOOOOO
MOO MOO MOO MOO MOO MOO, MOO MOO MOO MOO!

(*Back to the original tempo...*)

AHHHHHH, I LIKE THE WEST WHERE THE SKY IS BLUE!

MOO.

LANFORD & MARTHA.
YOU LIKE THE WEST AND THE WEST LIKES YOU!

COWS.
MOO.

LANFORD & MARTHA.
I'M GLAD THE WAR IS OVER, AND IT'S TIME TO START ANEW!

COWS. *(rising scale)*
NEW NEW NEW NEW NEWWWWWWWWW!

LANFORD & MARTHA.
WE LIKE THE WEST LIKE THE STARS LIKE THE MOON!

LANFORD & MARTHA & COWS. *(big finish)*
YESSSSSSSS! WE LIKE THE WEST LIKE THE STARS LIKE THE MOON!

(The **COWS** *low like real cows.)*

COWS. Moo. Moo. Moo. Moo.

*(**LANFORD** bows deeply, like **HENRY** did at the top of the play.)*

LANFORD. Good evening, Miss Martha.

MARTHA. Why, good heavens, Lanford! You look so…old.

LANFORD. I am old.

MARTHA. Why is that, I wonder?

LANFORD. I don't know. It just happened. One day I woke up old. Just like that. Say, did you have that baby yet?

MARTHA. Yeah, sure; he's in my trusty Calistoga there, doing his homework and darning my socks.

LANFORD. Uh huh.

COWS. Moo. Moo.

MARTHA. Oh, I'm so rude. Lanford, these are my faithful companions – Mother Milk Cow and her Calf.

LANFORD. How do you moo?

MOTHER COW. Moo.

CALF. Moo.

MARTHA. Shoo, shoo.

(She shoos her **COWS** *upstage, grabs something to sit on, and "lights" the campfire.)*

Shoot, give your weary dogs a rest and join me by the campfire, Lanford. How the heck have you been? Tell me your tales.

LANFORD. We moved to Chicago, Detroit and New York for a spell, but Henry never felt truly at home in the city. So we came out West, seeking our fortunes and fame.

MARTHA. Henry's dead, Lanford.

LANFORD. No, he's not. He's right here. I couldn't leave that big, lanky farm boy behind.

*(***LANFORD** *pats his suitcase.)*

MARTHA. You got Henry in a suitcase? Oh, Lanford.

*(***LANFORD** *opens his suitcase. Henry's bones are arrayed as if in a display case. He lovingly pulls several bones from the suitcase.)*

LANFORD. His leg bone. His arm bone. His finger bone with my wedding ring upon it.

MARTHA. You and Henry got hitched?

LANFORD. Ages ago.

MARTHA. You can't marry somebody who's dead.

LANFORD. *(a flat fact)* In my country you can marry who-ever you want.

MARTHA. Are you pulling my leg?

LANFORD. Nope.

MARTHA. *(privately)* What if you want to marry a cow? I ain't saying I do, but what if I did?

LANFORD. Love is all you need.

MARTHA. But what if it's a girl cow?

LANFORD. Girls, boys, cows, trees, water, grass, sky, red, yellow, purple, blue. All love is holy.

(...NFORD gets Henry's skull out and talks to it.)

...ORD. Ain't that right, Henry? Are you feeling holy tonight?

(to MARTHA*)*

There's no killing allowed in my country neither. We all live forever.

(He makes the skull talk.)

"Hi, Martha. How are you? I'm in a transcendental state."

CALF. *(played by* HENRY *actor)* Moo.

MARTHA. Put Henry's head back in the suitcase. You're giving me the creeps.

LANFORD. Henry's been very concerned about you and his baby. Ain't that right, Henry?

MARTHA. Henry's dead. He's not worried about anything, Lanford.

LANFORD. Henry is worried that somebody done put a spell on you.

MARTHA. Oh, you sound like a common yard darky.

LANFORD. You better hurry this labor along or you're gonna give birth to a teenager, woman!

MARTHA. You think I like getting up three, four times a night to answer nature's call? I'm hungry. My back hurts. I'm constantly in tears about inconsequential things. I can't wait for this kid to come out so I can have my body back! Yes, I'm scared, and yes, I admit, I'm a little picky and over-protective. But nobody wants this baby more than I do. I just have to find a safe place to raise it, that's all.

LANFORD. Henry and I have had a long, heartfelt talk about this, and we firmly believe you need to see a proper doctor.

MARTHA. A proper doctor let my mother bleed to death in childbirth.

LANFORD. Be that as it may, you cannot pretend you're not pregnant.

MARTHA. Oh, don't give me the Harvard trea Lanford. I know my condition! Thanks to Miste of Bones there, I know it in every fiber of my be every moment of my life. Having a baby is who I ar Lanford.

(suddenly verging on tears)

I know I'm not normal. I've always known that. I just want my kid to have a better shake than I did.

LANFORD. I know.

MARTHA. I know you know. And you know what makes me the maddest?

LANFORD. What?

MARTHA. Maybe my father was right. That son of a bitch used to come home from church and beat the day-lights outa me – but maybe Pa was right. Maybe I shoulda stayed on that train and given this child away to a good Christian home. Maybe I ain't fit to raise it. Maybe that's why God don't want me to birth it.

LANFORD. I think you'll make a fine mama. You just have to give yourself a chance.

MOTHER COW. Moo. Moo.

MARTHA. I know, I know. I've been in a state of continuous expectation for too long, you're right.

CALF. Moo.

LANFORD. *(makes* **HENRY***'s skull talk)* "Martha, we love you and care about you and the baby."

(as **LANFORD***)*

Now will you please let us take you to a doctor?

COWS. *(it's a good idea)* Moo. Moo.

MARTHA. *(after a moment…)* I ain't seeing a man doctor. I don't want some stupid know-it-all poking his grimy doctor hands around in my private places who has no idea what I'm going through.

LANFORD. I don't know as there are any female doctors. Henry, you heard of a lady doc? "Nope."

A. Would you either bury that poor man or put
him back to rest in his ratty old suitcase?! No offense,
Henry, but you really do give me the creeps.

LANFORD. Say good night, Henry.

(as **HENRY***)*

"Good night, Martha. Good luck with the baby."

*(***LANFORD** *lovingly puts Henry's bones back in the suitcase.)*

MARTHA. You can't keep dragging your love life around
like this, Lanford.

(The cows amble over to bid her farewell.)

CALF. Moo. Moo.

MOTHER COW. Moo. Moo.

MARTHA. Thank you. I'll miss you two, too.

MARTHA & COWS. *(saying goodbye)* Moo. Moo. Moo. Moo.

(etc.)

LANFORD. Alright then – it's time to board the birthing
train!

(We hear a steam engine whistle.)

MARTHA. What birthing train?

*(Projections of black and white railroad movie images,
from early in the 20th century, appear on the upstage
wall or scrim.)*

LANFORD. Just follow us down to the railroad tracks, sister!
The future is right over yon! Alllllll Aboard!

*(***LANFORD** *moves his arm in a circle. Maybe the suitcase
puffs smoke.* **MARTHA** *falls in behind* **LANFORD** *and his
suitcase as the projections meld with buffalo and cattle
and cowboys and indians and wagon trains, etc. Music
underscores.)*

MARTHA. Fare thee well, faithful bovines. I'm setting you
free to roam the range with the buffalo, if'n there's
any left. Moo!

COWS. Moo. Moo. Moo. Moo.

(MARTHA and LANFORD exit. The COWS turn upste
and watch for a moment, as if they're at a drive-in movie
on the prairie.)

(They exit as we hear an old-time phone ringing, circa
1917.)

(NURSE SINGER enters in full-on period clothing, a
white uniform and little cap. She answers her ringing
phone. NURSE SINGER doesn't need to change her voice
to be female, just her attitude. If the actor playing her
has a beard, then so does she. The only furniture in her
office is an old metal chair or stool.)

NURSE SINGER. Oh, that infernal ringing!

(answers the phone)

Hello? Nurse Singer speaking. Oh, fine, Operator, put
her through.

(MARTHA and LANFORD slowly enter. He uses a cane
and is much, much older now. They stare at the phone.)

NURSE SINGER. (cont.) It's my mother. Excuse me.

(back to phone)

Yes, Mama, what is it now?

(listens)

Then drink a Coca-Cola and go lie down if you have a
migraine. Mama, I can't talk right now. I'm with a new
patient. Goodbye. Thank you, Operator, bye-bye.

(hangs up)

Now. What can I do for you, child?

LANFORD. Miss Martha's in a…family way, Ma'am.

MARTHA. (crosses to the phone) You can talk to your mama
with that contraption?

NURSE SINGER. There's no colored allowed in here, boy.

MARTHA. He's not colored, Ma'am. Lanford's Eye-talian.

NURSE SINGER. And I'm the Queen of England. Go on,
boy. You wait out back in the alley.

No. I want Lanford to stay here with me.

SINGER. Young lady, We are going to be concerning ourselves with very private personal female matters.

NFORD. It's fine, Miss Martha, I'll be right outside. You tell the nurse everything about your condition now. Don't hold nothing back.

(**MARTHA** *helps* **LANFORD** *to the door without really "helping" him – he's prideful – he's also the slowest walker in the world.*)

MARTHA. Don't wait in the alley, OK? You set out front on a bench in the sunlight.

(*privately*)

Lanford, do you need to visit the privy? You gonna be OK for a little spell?

LANFORD. Will you quit yammering about my bladder? I emptied my bladder 'fore we got here. I feel good just knowing you're finally in the right place.

(*sort of yells at his suitcase*)

Ain't that right, Henry?

(**LANFORD** *exits.* **MARTHA** *turns back to the* **NURSE.**)

MARTHA. Lord. He is so touchy and prideful. You know how men get at that age.

NURSE SINGER. Where on God's earth do you hail from, child?

MARTHA. Look Out, Kentucky.

NURSE SINGER. Do your parents know you're clear out here to New Mexico?

MARTHA. No, Ma'am, my mother's deceased, and my pa threw me out of the house.

NURSE SINGER. Oh, you poor thing you. How far along are you?

MARTHA. You're gonna think I'm crazy if'n I tell you the truth.

NURSE SINGER. Sweet Pea, I am not here to judge. There ain't much I ain't seen. You have a problem. I'm here to help.

MARTHA. *(suddenly verging on tears)* I just want to m.. my baby's healthy and everything's going OK there.

NURSE SINGER. *(gives her hanky)* Of course you do.

MARTHA. I just get so worried it won't be born normal. I mean I'm gonna love it no matter what, but I've been pregnant for a coon's age, and…good Lord, I'm weepy.

NURSE SINGER. Everybody feels that way. Now. When's the last time Aunt Flow came to visit?

MARTHA. Right after the War started. My beau joined Army and I thought I loved him, and I just wanted him to remember me, I guess. It was the first time for both of us.

NURSE SINGER. Does the baby's daddy know he's gonna be a daddy?

MARTHA. He did, but he died in the War.

NURSE SINGER. Was he over to France? Was it that awful mustard gas that got him?

MARTHA. No, Ma'am, he died in Maryland. Just outside Sharpsburg.

NURSE SINGER. You must be confused.

(**NURSE SINGER** *listens to* **MARTHA***'s belly with a stethoscope.*)

MARTHA. I do feel confused, but it's been so long. What year is it now?

NURSE SINGER. 1917. When's your birthday, dear? I know you're young. There's no need to be ashamed.

MARTHA. March 7th….1845.

(*The* **NURSE** *stares, but betrays no reaction.*)

Do you think I'm touched by evil spirits?

NURSE SINGER. No.

MARTHA. Cause I feel like I'm still sixteen, but the world just keeps rushing by me so fast. I mean Lanford got so old, and poor Henry bought the farm, but he still keeps him in a suitcase – and it's all going faster and faster the older I get, but like I just told you, I'm not getting older.

SINGER. You look sixteen to me.

MARTHA. Have you ever in all your born days had a patient stay pregnant as long as me?

NURSE SINGER. Sweet Pea, if what you're telling me is true –

MARTHA. It is.

NURSE SINGER. – you would be seventy two years old now.

MARTHA. I am, but I'm not! It's just queer as cabbage.

NURSE SINGER. Will you excuse me a moment?

MARTHA. Ma'am?

NURSE SINGER. Yes?

MARTHA. You do believe me, don't you?

NURSE SINGER. Of course I do.

MARTHA. I know full well it sounds like a stretcher, but it ain't. Time gets all stretchy, but I'm not stretching anything. I'm telling the God's honest truth.

NURSE SINGER. Honey, I told you, I'm here to help.

(**NURSE SINGER** *gets a brass key out and "locks the door" as she exits.*)

MARTHA. What are you doing? Nurse Singer, why are you locking the door?

(*exits, tries the "door," re-enters*)

Oh, crap. I knew I shoulda kept my ignorant mouth shut. Lanford?? Lanford, are you out there?? Can you hear me?? Oh, Lord love a goose…

(*She goes to the phone, picks it up, and tries to make it work.*)

Hello? Mother? Mother, can you hear me? Is anybody there? Operator? Mama? Can you hear me? Can somebody help me please? Help!!!

(*Whereupon,* **NURSE SINGER** *enters with a* **PSYCHIATRIC AIDE,** *played by the Lanford actor. They have a straight jacket.*)

NURSE SINGER. Hold out your arms and slip this little jacket on, Sweet Pea.

MARTHA. What for?

NURSE SINGER. It's a special female examination co… help you keep your modesty, dear.

MARTHA. I don't think I like this.

PSYCHIATRIC AIDE. You'll feel much better when you get to the hospital.

NURSE SINGER. Hold still. Now, now. Don't upset the baby.

MARTHA. Hey. Hey. Hey. Stop! I'm not crazy! I'm pregnant!

(Lights snap to black. Music swirls backwards [like revolution number #9*], full of voices/sounds echoing moments from the play, which crescendo into a buzzing electronic sound, and…)*

(Lights up on **DOCTOR KLINGGINHOFFER**. *He speaks into a period microphone. White coat, glasses, notebook. His voice comes through speakers…like God on a school P.A. system. The idea is that he's addressing a medical theatre full of psychiatric interns.)*

KLINGGINHOFFER. Ze psychodynamic cause of ze delusional or hysterical pregnancy is alvays, alvays rooted in childhood trauma. Howsomever, in zis case, ze loss of ze mother at an early age causes ze patient to idealize her mother. Zis psychosomatic transference along vith ze contiguous discovery of ze lack of ze phallus in ze patient causes ze envy of ze penis in ze father.

*(***MARTHA** *enters in a straight jacket and hospital gown standing next to* **MARY**, *another pregnant patient, also in a straight jacket and gown.)*

MARTHA. I swear I can't understand a word that man says.

MARY. He says you got penis envy.

MARTHA. Doctor Klingginhoffer, I don't pine for extra equipment. And by the way, you can write down in your little notebook I hated my father's guts.

MARY. You really shouldn't've said that.

MARTHA. I thought we were supposed to be honest here, Mary.

(*correcting*) Virgin Mary.

GGINHOFFER. Ze Electra complex leads ze daughter to fantasize zat she has become pregnant by her own father.

MARY. Works for me. I became pregnant by my heavenly father.

KLINGGINHOFFER. Ze female has a veak superego, and all vomen envy ze penis.

MARY. He says all women envy –

MARTHA. With all due respect, Doctor Klingginhoffer, that's just a big stinking load of horse hockey. I don't envy anybody's penis. I don't want a penis, I don't like thinking about penises and I especially hate having to sit here talking about em when we could be talking about something useful – like when are you going to let me out of the booby hatch?

MARY. Don't count your chickens.

MARTHA. Shut up, Mary.

MARY. Virgin Mary.

KLINGGINHOFFER. Ze lobotomy or ze electric shock treatment for ze Electra complex? Zat is ze question. Vether tis shmarter and nobler to suffer ze zings and ze zaps of ze elctro shock therapy treatment – or to shtick ze lobotomy instrument into ze brain und cut avay ze delusional tissue.

(*Lights "sizzle" and zap out on* **KLINGGINHOFFER**. *Music melds into* **KLINGGINHOFFER**'s *P.A. announcements for the asylum – things like same-sex square dancing and mandatory arts and craft therapy.*)

(*Lights up on* **MARY** *and* **MARTHA** *in the craft lounge, minus their straight jackets.* **MARTHA** *sews on a simple rag doll.* **MARY** *wears a white T-shirt on her head, like the Virgin or a nun.* **SADIE**, *another pregnant patient, sits in a chair – comatose…she never moves. A male* **PSYCHIATRIC AIDE** *lounges in a wheel chair, smoking…*)

MARY. Electra, Electra, who cares about the dumb [
Complex besides you and Doctor Klingginho[
"Oh, I've been with child since 1861." "Oh, gee, t[
Civil War was hard on me." "Oh, mercy, I don't have
a penis."

MARTHA. Mary –

MARY. Virgin Mary.

MARTHA. Let's sew our craft projects in silence, OK?

MARY. 1861…Try zero. Try I've been with child since zero.
It all starts with me. And *my* baby.

MARTHA. OK, fine.

MARY. Zero.

(pause)

MARY. *(cont.)* When I told my fiancé, Joseph, about what
happened to me – I said I'm pregnant, Joseph, but
don't worry because I'm still a virgin. God did it.
Really, I didn't go out behind the stable and copulate
with anyone else. It was God. I was sleeping, I woke up
pregnant, just like that. I said I'm saving myself for you
and holy marriage like a good girl. And do you know
what Joseph said to me, Martha?

PSYCHIATRIC AIDE. Yeah, he said you're outa your fucking
mind.

MARY. He said, Mary, you're still my girl.

(Silence. They sew.)

MARTHA. *(kindly)* You know my mother's name was Mary.

MARY. Not Virgin Mary.

MARTHA. Just plain Mary. Mary Martha.

MARY. That's sweet. What are you sewing on?

MARTHA. Just a rag doll.

MARY. Oh.

MARTHA. When I was little I had a doll like this. Since I
didn't have a mother, I used to pretend the doll was
my mother. I'd tell myself stories and ask my doll to
sing me a lullaby.

I knew a girl who used to pretend that she slept with two boys from the colored high school football team at the same time, and then one day it happened. Her daddy did unspeakable things to those boys, then he took her to the looney bin and he won't ever never ever let her out. Why doesn't Doctor Klingginhoffer pay attention to me???

PYSCHIATRIC AIDE. You're scheduled for electroshock therapy this afternoon.

MARY. *(pleased, but worried)* I am? He's gonna shock me?

PYSCHIATRIC AIDE. Uh huh.

MARY. Doctor Klingginhoffer himself?

PYSCHIATRIC AIDE. Uh huh. He shocked Sadie last week. She's doing good now, ain't that so, Sadie?

MARTHA. She don't speak at all no more.

PYSCHIATRIC AIDE. No, but she don't scream and cry no more neither. Hey, Virgin, you want to have sex before your shock treatment? I'll give you a cigarette for a blow job.

MARTHA. I swear, if you do that, I'll scream from the tree tops.

PYSCHIATRIC AIDE. You do that, they'll give you a shock treatment, too.

MARY. I'm saving myself for Doctor Klingginhoffer.

*(Whereupon, a buzzer sounds and **KLINGGINHOFFER** enters in his lab coat.)*

KLINGGINHOFFER. Zer she is. Zer's za Virgin Mary. How are ve feeling zis afternoon?

MARY. Good. A little nervous, but –

KLINGGINHOFFER. And are ve ready for our electroconvulsive shock therapy treatment?

MARY. I don't know. I've never done anything like –

KLINGGINHOFFER. Zer's nothing to be afraid of. Zer is no pain from ze electroshock.

*(The **AIDE** and **KLINGGINHOFFER** guide **MARY** into a wheelchair, as:)*

MARY. If you think it's for the best.

KLINGGINHOFFER. I do, I do.

MARY. Doctor Klingginhoffer, what does the electricity do? Will it cure me?

KLINGGINHOFFER. Yes, it vill help vith your neurosis. Ve use it to treat sexual deviancy, homosexuality, bestiality, pedophilia, depression, alcoholism, and delusionary behavior.

MARY. I just slept with a black boy is all.

PSYCHIATRIC AIDE. Two black boys, Mary.

MARY. Good bye, Martha. Good luck with the baby.

MARTHA. You, too.

MARY. Bye, Sadie.

(And they're gone. A long beat of silence, then the buzzing hummmmm of electricity fills the theatre. Lights surge and dim. Then, comatose SADIE *says:)*

SADIE. Moooooooo.

(Thunder. SADIE *exits. Tight light on* MARTHA *holding her rag doll.)*

MARTHA. Mama? I'm scared. I feel like I'm cursed, and the world keeps getting worse. I can't sleep, I can't think...I don't understand why they're keeping me here. I know I'm with child. I'm not insane.

(She makes the doll "tall")

MARTHA/ RAG DOLL. You're talking to a rag doll.

MARTHA. Shut up.

MARTHA/ RAG DOLL. Don't take that tone with your mother.

MARTHA. I got to get out of here before they stick knives in my brain or shock me and make me forget my own name. I might be a little bit bat shit, but that's not his fault. Or hers.

(privately, a little fragile)

I sorta think it's a girl, Ma. They say boys sit up high and girls sit down low, right? Or is it the way around?

THA/ RAG DOLL. Whatever it is, you cannot give birth in the looney bin, Martha.

MARTHA. You think I don't know that?

MARTHA/ RAG DOLL. Quit talking to yourself.

MARTHA. Shut up.

MARTHA/ RAG DOLL. You shut up.

MARTHA. You shut up. Ahhhh!

(**MARTHA** *throws the rag doll on the floor, stands up.*)

Doctor Klingginhoffer? Doc, I know you're observing me. Can't you just give me an X-ray or test me or do whatever you gotta do to prove that I'm living for two now? Cause if I'm not...then I swear to God, I'll climb on that table and strap myself down, Doctor Klingginhoffer.

(beat)

Doctor Klingginhoffer? Can you hear me?

(An efficient **LADY ADMINISTRATOR** *enters with a clipboard.)*

LADY ADMINISTRATOR. Doctor Klingginhoffer's not here any more, Martha.

MARTHA. What do you mean?

LADY ADMINISTRATOR. He's been drafted.

(Projection of a slow-motion waving American flag on the upstage wall, and the faint sound of the song "Over There" in the background, as:)

LADY ADMINISTRATOR. *(cont.)* According to our records, you have no source of income or verifiable means of support. Which makes you a burden to the taxpayers.

MARTHA. What do you mean?

LADY ADMINISTRATOR. Martha, we are at war. Patriotic Americans have far more pressing concerns than supporting a single mother-to-be who wants to feed at the public trough.

MARTHA. Does that mean you're letting me out of the booby hatch?

LADY ADMINISTRATOR. Yes.

MARTHA. Thank you.

LADY ADMINISTRATOR. You're welcome. Next?

MARTHA. Sir? I mean Ma'am?

LADY ADMINISTRATOR. Yes?

MARTHA. Who are we at war with now?

LADY ADMINISTRATOR. Germany. Japan.

MARTHA. We just barely got done fighting with Germany. Who won?

LADY ADMINISTRATOR. We did.

MARTHA. Then why are we fighting 'em again?

LADY ADMINISTRATOR. Go to church. Get married. Buy a house. Have children. Get a job. Pay taxes. Buy bonds. Support the troops. Next!

(Music builds. Screen image…the atom bomb exploding with **MARTHA** *standing before it, watching.)*

(A **CARNIVAL BARKER** *enters, twirling a cane.)*

BARKER. Step right up, folks! Don't be shy! Try your luck! Stump the Amazing All-American Bible Girl. Pick a verse! Name a verse! Any verse at all! Just one dollar, friends. Step right up, try your luck.

(A " **MARK** *" steps up.)*

MARK. I think today is my lucky day.

MARTHA. Name your verse.

MARK. Uh, Proverbs. Chapter 22. Verse 6, please

BARKER. Forwards or backwards?

MARK. Well…

BARKER. Backwards is ten to one odds.

MARK. OK.

MARTHA. Period. It From Depart Not Will He Old Is He When And Lord The Of Ways The In Child A Up Train. "Train up a child in the ways of the Lord and when he is old he will not depart from it. Period."

MARK. Prostituting God's word for profit. You must be very proud.

(The **MARK** *exits.)*

BARKER. Step right up! Don't be shy, people! Stump the Amazing All American Bible girl!

(We hear the "DING" of an airplane. Cloud projections on the upstage wall. Lights up on a **STEWARDESS,** *dressed in a "60's" miniskirt and high heeled boots.* **MARTHA** *sits down in a chair, which serves as her seat on the plane.)*

STEWARDESS. Welcome to American Airlines. Fasten your seat belts and lock your tray-tables in place for take off, please.

*(***STEWARDESS** *produces a demo oxygen mask.)*

In case of emergency fasten the mask securely over your face and breathe normally. Thank you for flying American.

(The **STEWARDESS** *sits in her "jump seat" as the plane noises build, the clouds fly by faster, and the "plane" takes off.)*

MARTHA. Oh, my God. Oh, my God. Whoa, Nelly!

*(***MARTHA** *pokes her finger at the airplane "ceiling." Four dings, and an oxygen mask drops down from above.* **MARTHA** *grabs it, puts it on and breathes. After a moment, the* **STEWARDESS** *crosses to her.)*

STEWARDESS. Excuse me? Miss? What are you doing?

MARTHA. Breathing!

(She breathes.)

Oh! Hooo! Hoo! Oh. My. That's better. Hoo. I tell you, this woulda come in right handy at Antietam. I couldn't breathe, I couldn't think, I couldn't find the ground for the bodies upon it. I can't begin to tell you how many just plain breathing emergencies I've had in my day.

STEWARDESS. Are you all right, Miss?

MARTHA. Ma'am? Where are we going?

STEWARDESS. *(with attitude)* San Francisco. Where else?

(Cue a 1960s rock tune, something along the lines of MAGIC CARPET RIDE.*)

*(San Francisco, 1969. **THREE HIPPIES** share a joint. You can't tell if they're boys or girls, except for **BETTY**, who is in a miniskirt and stripper boots.)*

BETTY. Whoa.

FLOWER. Heavy.

SUNSHINE. This is good shit.

FLOWER. I am so fucking fucked up I can't fucking tell you how fucking high I am. Fuck me! I am fucked the fuck up!

*(**MARTHA** enters, or crosses into the scene. She wears a Union Army jacket over her blood-stained dress. She carries a small suitcase, the one with **HENRY**'s bones in a it. She fits right in.)*

MARTHA. Hi.

FLOWER. Yes, I am.

BETTY. Oh, man, I love that whole like retro Army look.

SUNSHINE. I don't like the military, but I do dig the statement, man.

BETTY. You've got a whole groovy kinda thing going on, baby. What's your name, baby?

MARTHA. Martha.

FLOWER. Where'd you get those clothes, Martha?

MARTHA. From the Union.

SUNSHINE. Oh, that's a cool store.

BETTY. You want to get stoned, Martha?

MARTHA. You mean like Mary Magdalene?

FLOWER. Fuck me. That's heavy. That's fucking poetry.

SUNSHINE. What's in the suitcase?

MARTHA. My dead lover's bones and his dead lover's wedding ring.

HIPPIES. Whoa…!!! *(etc.)*

---

* Please see Music Use Note on Page 3

LOWER. Intense. You are like…karmic, man.

MARTHA. I don't mean to pry, but are you boys or girls?

FLOWER. Like what do you want me to be? I'm open minded. I dig the vast scene.

BETTY. We're living on love, baby. Boys and girls and girls and boys and boys and boys and girls and girls.

SUNSHINE. It's all good, baby.

MARTHA. Lanford would have loved this place.

(**MARTHA** *is holding the joint.*)

BETTY. Martha?

MARTHA. Yes?

BETTY. *(wants the joint back)* That's not a microphone. Share the wealth, baby.

(*She gives* **BETTY** *the joint.* **HANK/STAGEHAND** *brings on a microphone on a stand. Sets it down and exits.*)

FLOWER. Whoa. Now *that* is a microphone.

(*Music. Huge guitar chords augmented by the violin. A heavy 60's solo. Projections from San Francisco's Summer of Love on the screen.* **MARTHA** *steps up to the microphone and sings, Janis Joplin-like.*)

MARTHA. *(sings)*
BREAK ME, SHAKE ME, TAKE ME,
DON'T FORSAKE ME
MAKE ME YOURS, SAN FRANCISCO.
HOLD ME, SHIELD ME,
LOVE ME, HEAL ME
FEEL THE SPIRIT OF LOVE ALL AROUND YOU
SAN FRANCISCO, LET YOUR LOVE RAIN
DOWN ON ME.

HIPPIES. *(sing back-up)*
HOO, HOO. HOO, HOO. HOO, HOO. (ETC.)

MARTHA.
I GOT A HUNGER THAT WON'T LEAVE ME ALONE
I WANDERED ALL ACROSS THIS LAND TO MAKE THIS PLACE
MY HOME.

AND I GOT A HURT THAT ONLY YOU CAN HEAL
TOUCH ME, TAKE ME, LOVE ME, WAKE ME,
MAKE ME FEEL REAL.

MARTHA & HIPPIES.

SAN FRANCISCO, SAN FRANCISCO,
SAN FRANCISCO
LET YOUR LOVE RAIN DOWN ON ME.
SAN FRANCISCO, SAN FRANCISCO,
SAN FRANCISCO
LET YOUR LOVE RAIN DOWN ON ME.

MARTHA. *(as Hippies contniue San Francisco chorus in b.g.)*

I BELIEVE IN HOPE
I BELIEVE IN MAGIC
I BELIEVE IN LOVE SWEET LOVE
RAIN DOWN ON ME.

I BELIEVE IN PEACE
I BELIEVE IN MUSIC
I BELIEVE IN LOVE SWEET LOVE
RAIN DOWN ON ME
LOVE RAIN DOWN ON ME
LOVE RAIN DOWN ON ME

MARTHA. *(big Joplin-esque finish)*

LOOOOVE RAAAAIN DOOOOWN ONNNN MEEEEEEEEE.

*(HANK enters from the audience, dressed in bell bottom jeans with a military jacket or shirt. He climbs on stage. **HIPPIES** exit, taking microphones with them.)*

HANK. You are the coolest girl on the planet, man. When you sing, you lift off like a rocket – I'm not kidding, you levitate, man. Is that a bird? Is that a plane? Is it Superchick? No, man – it's you. Like where did you come from?

MARTHA. Kentucky.

HANK. Right on, man! Like I'm from Kentucky, too.

MARTHA. I'll be dogged.

HANK. What are you doing out here?

MARTHA. My dad threw me out of the house.

HANK. Are you kidding? Me, too!

MARTHA. Your dad threw you out, too?

HANK. Like I got in a beef with the police back in Louisville cause they found a roach in my ashtray and two pounds of herb in the trunk of my old man's Corvair – I had no choice, man – they made me enlist and shipped me off to 'nam, even though I'd just burned my draft card.

MARTHA. Right on.

HANK. Next thing I know, I'm in the fricking jungle, stoned off my ass, when the commies start popping off rounds at us, right? My Captain says, "Hank, crawl down that tunnel and shoot me some gooks."

MARTHA. Your name's Hank?

HANK. My real name's Henry, but Hank's what I go by – so I'm not about to crawl down this rabbit hole and shoot a bunch of peasants I got nothing against. So you know what I did?

MARTHA. What?

HANK. I told my Captain I'm gay.

(then)

You should have seen the look on his face! I said, "Sir, I am so flaming queer, I want to kiss you right now on the lips, Captain."

MARTHA. Really?

HANK. So they shipped me back to the states, gave me a dishonorable discharge, my old man kicked me out, I stuck out my thumb, and here I am making the scene in Frisco, man. How cool is that?

MARTHA. Wow. So are you?

HANK. Do I look like I play for the other team?

MARTHA. Everybody looks like they play for the other team, Hank.

(beat)

HANK. Can I ask you a personal question? Like where is your boyfriend?

MARTHA. I don't have a boyfriend, Hank.

HANK. Really? Me neither.

(off her smile)

So, Martha from Kentucky. You need a place to crash?

(Lights up on Hank's apartment. It feels like the inside of a lava lamp. One chair, a small table. If need be, the back up singers can carry the furniture on while reprising the "SAN FRANCISCO" chorus.)

HIPPIES. *(sing softly, romantically)*:

SAN FRANCISCO, SAN FRANCISCO

SAN FRANCISCO

LET YOUR LOVE RAIN DOWN ON ME.

(HANK lights a candle and a joint.)

HANK. My pad is your pad.

MARTHA. It's mighty kind of you to take in a wayfaring stranger.

HANK. You can't sleep on the streets, Martha. I mean you're like…you know.

MARTHA. Like pregnant.

HANK. Yeah. You want to get high?

MARTHA. I'm good, thanks.

HANK. You care if I partake?

MARTHA. No. You know my dad used to read me the Bible by candle light.

HANK. Have you read the Karma Sutra?

MARTHA. The karma who?

HANK. The whole Hindu Buddhist Eastern gig, man. Like we've all been here before, can you dig it? You should read *Zen and the Art of Motorcycle Maintenance*, man. That'll blow your mind.

MARTHA. Really?

HANK. Like right now – right this second, I feel like I've known you before.

MARTHA. I feel like we've met before, too, Hank.

HANK. This is so radical! Shit. So like who do you think your baby used to be? In a previous life.

MARTHA. I don't know, but I think it's got a really old soul.

HANK. What if it's Jesus, man?

MARTHA. Jesus?

HANK. How fricking cool would that be? Like what if your baby's the light of the world?

MARTHA. That is the nicest thing anyone's ever said to me.

HANK. This is really good shit, man. You sure you don't want some?

MARTHA. I'm kinda getting a contact high just from being with you, Hank.

HANK. You want to go bed with me, Martha?

(off her hesitation)

It's cool, man, I'm sorry – like you're in a delicate state. You take the bed, man, I'll just grab some blankets and stuff and crash out on the…

MARTHA. I don't know why you'd want to sleep with some-body who's big as a house.

HANK. Are you kidding me, man? You look great. You got this whole curvy, fleshy, earth mother groove going, Martha. I'm not kidding – you radiate life, man – your skin is clear, plus, your boobs are kinda…

MARTHA. Swollen. And tender.

HANK. Hey, I'm all about tender. We don't have to mess around or anything. We can just, you know…hold onto each other and slip into dreamland.

MARTHA. What if I want to mess around?

HANK. That just makes the dreamland trip all that much better, man.

(He wraps the blanket around them both, à la that photo from Woodstock.)

Martha?

MARTHA. Hank?

HANK. You've got a boyfriend now, man.

(As they kiss, we hear a reprise of the waltz from the opening scene. Stars appear. They sink to the floor and make out for awhile in the soft romantic light...)

MARTHA. Oh, Hank, I'm so glad I found you.

(kisses him)

I feel like we're young again. Like I can breathe again finally.

HANK. Oh, man...Martha, baby...the sun's almost up...you know what that means?

MARTHA. We get to mess around in the daylight.

HANK. I gotta get to work, baby.

MARTHA. Just stay here and hold me. Let's make out all day and tell each other every single secret we have.

HANK. If I'm late one more time, my boss is gonna kill me.

MARTHA. Just stay for an hour. Please.

HANK. I can't...I gotta go.

MARTHA. Half an hour – ten minutes – ten kisses – just ten more kisses.

HANK. *(overlapping)* I gotta go to work.

*(**HANK** rolls away from her. The lights change to morning, as he crosses off for a second to grab a suit and tie.)*

MARTHA. I'm gonna wait for you, Hank. I'll clean our apartment and make a nice dinner and then when you get home, we'll –

HANK. Whoa, whoa, whoa – you can't stay here, man. We spent one night together. Wake up.

*(**HANK** changes out of his bell bottom jeans and into a suit and tie during the following.)*

MARTHA. But you said our baby's the light of the –

HANK. Our baby? Jesus Christ – what are you on? Martha – baby – look, you're a nice girl, we had a little fun, but I don't need some runaway chick hanging around my apartment all day playing house, alright?

MARTHA. Henry –

HANK. I told you, I go by Hank. Jesus. Don't cry, kid. I'm sorry. But what did you think was gonna happen here? We shack up one time, and poof – instant family? I work fast, but not that fast, man. Jesus, I'm late. The stock exchange opened two hours ago.

MARTHA. I killed for you, Henry. I carried your moldy old bones across hell and high water. I even took care of your incontinent boyfriend.

HANK. Whatever you're on, man, I hope you come down off it soon.

MARTHA. I thought you were different. I thought you'd changed.

HANK. Martha, the only thing that's changing right now is the international exchange rate, okay? The dollar's down, the yen is up, and the yields are fucking outrageous. Why do they always put starch in my – ? Fuck it, man, I gotta score some coke, grab a cab, and – what did I do with my cell phone? Have you seen my cell?

MARTHA. No.

HANK. Where is my fucking BlackBerry?!? Christ.

(finds it in his pocket)

There it is. There you are. There's my little life-line. Look, I'd love to hang out and do the whole capuccino-croissant-meaningful-morning-after-talk thing, but… Jesus Christ, Google just shot through the fucking roof. Oh, my God. Oh, my God. It doesn't get any better than this! I gotta go, baby. Shoot me a text, we'll hook up some time.

MARTHA. Hank? Is that true?

HANK. Absolutely.

MARTHA. Henry. Hank. Wait. It really truly doesn't get any better than this?

HANK. Are you kidding me? Right here, right now. This is as good it gets, kid. Good luck with the baby.

(He exits. Hold for a beat, then the "TV" clicks ON. We hear news reports; **MARTHA** *is bathed in flickering light as images are projected on the upstage screen/scrim... stock market reports, Desert Storm, McVeigh bombing the federal building in Oklahoma –* **MARTHA** *clicks to the war in Kosovo, then to Colorado school shootings, then to 9-11 news, planes flying into the World Trade Center, people jumping out of the towers, etc. She clicks faster and faster as the news melds with music, growing more and more surreal, poetic, mournful and frightening... Afghanistan, Bin Laden, shock and awe, Abu Ghraib, Guantanamo, the Madrid train station bombing, the Mumbai massacre, Gaza invasion, etc., etc....building to present tense madness. At the same time, a blanket of fog is slowly rolling across the stage. After 60 seconds of this at the most, building and building:)*

*(***LANFORD*** enters dressed in his Civil War era uniform. He takes the remote out of* **MARTHA***'s hand, and clicks the TV off. The only sound now is music. Lights change.* **LANFORD** *speaks to the theatre.)*

LANFORD. Once our dear Martha determined that this world would never be a fit place to bring forth her child, she was left with no choice: she took Henry's remains and hiked out to the cliffs high above San Francisco. Marin County. Where old hippies go to find God. Cliffs. Ocean. Fog and sky. Whereupon, Martha determined to fling herself and the child within off the high cliff and into the face of beauty itself – with one quick stop to be dashed on the rocks far below.

*(***MARTHA*** has crossed downstage with the suitcase. Lights isolate her. There are stars and two perfect round moons in the night sky.)*

She looked down at the sea, and she longed for the cold eternal embrace of the waves; and then she looked up at the eyes of her mother, shining like two perfect moons.

(Music becomes the voice of her mother.)

MARTHA. Ma, I keep thinking the world's gonna change, or I'll learn how to handle things better – but every time I get my shit together, somebody flies a plane into a building, or breaks my heart into a million little shadows the same way they broke it before. I don't expect to end up in the good place with you, unless God's been asleep. So here's what I'm asking: Mama, will you please look out for my baby? Tell the angels to sing her a lullaby. And you take her perfect little pinkish-white hand in yours, and tell her I loved with all my heart, Mama, the same way I know you loved me.

LANFORD. She took one last deep breath, filling herself with the courage to leap; and then she thought:

MARTHA. Don't you presume to know what I'm thinking. You don't have a clue about me.

LANFORD. I'm transcended, Martha. Is that a clue?

MARTHA. You're transcended, Lanford? Does that mean I'm dead now?

(**AMBROSE** *enters in period costume. His night shirt and robe.*)

AMBROSE. Not unless you commit the mortal sin of suicide.

MARTHA. What are you doing here, Pa?

AMBROSE. I'm transcended, too.

LANFORD. You are poised on the precipice betwixt life and death, Martha – which puts you squarely in touch with your deep inner cesspool.

AMBROSE. Romans! Chapter 3, verse 23!

MARTHA. Fuck you.

AMBROSE. "For all have sinned, and – "

MARTHA & AMBROSE. " – come short of the glory of God – "

MARTHA. – Pa, I know.

AMBROSE. Including me, Martha. I did the best I could, but we're all fallen fruit from the Tree of Life, daughter.

(**HENRY** *enters in his Home Militia uniform.*)

HENRY. Not me, Reverend. I sing the body electric. Hi, Lanford.

LANFORD. Hi, Henry.

AMBROSE. Why they let you people marry is beyond me.

LANFORD. *(smiles)* Fuck you.

HENRY. *(bows deeply)* Good evening, Miss Martha. Don't you look pretty?

MARTHA. Oh, stuff a sock in it, Henry.

HENRY. You may not believe this, but I always did love you.

(*to* **LANFORD**)

And you, too.

AMBROSE. Does nothing mean anything anymore? Dogs lie down with cats. Surely, the time of Revelation is at hand.

(**PRIMBODY** *enters, dressed in period clothing.*)

PRIMBODY. This whole Emancipation All Men Are Equal horse shit led to a terrifying birth of freedom, Pastor. Not to mention it put a mighty bad crimp in my runaway slave retrieval business.

(*sees* **LANFORD**)

Dante!

(*The* **MEN** *"morph" from character to character, sometimes within the same speech...*)

LANFORD. Hi, Primbody. Farmer.

HENRY. *(nods)* Cow. Dr. Klingginhoffer.

AMBROSE. Mary. Nurse Singer.

PRIMBODY. Hey, Betty, how they hanging, dude?

AMBROSE. Zis vould be ze envy of ze penis.

LANFORD. Atten-hut!

(*The* **MEN** *salute.*)

PRIMBODY. At ease, boys. And God save the Union...whatever that means.

AMBROSE. God save my daughter, sir. God save the child.

MARTHA. Look, gentleman. Ladies.

(*The* **MEN** *curtsy quickly.* **MARTHA** *spins upstage to confront them.*)

MARTHA. I'm not scared of dying. And I don't think it's fair to A) leave my baby to grow up a motherless waif, and/ or B) get born just in time for the ice caps to melt. And if you don't think that's gonna lead to a whole new slate of killing and weather and water and food wars, you didn't learn nothing from the carnage we wrought at Antietam.

LANFORD. This, despite the fact that a black man is president.

MARTHA. Oh, shut up, he is not.

LANFORD. He was. And soon after him a Republican lesbian got the job.

HENRY. Really? A lesbian? Really? What year is it?

LANFORD. Soon, Henry. It's soon now.

PRIMBODY. What's a lesbian?

AMBROSE. I miss the Culture Wars.

HENRY. I bet you do, Reverend.

PRIMBODY. I still miss Dante.

LANFORD. Moo.

HENRY. Moo.

AMBROSE. Moo.

PRIMBODY. Moo.

(*They moo softly as* **MARTHA** *has crosses back to the edge of the downstage "cliff.")*

(*The* **MEN** *close their eyes as if to pray,* **MARTHA** *closes her eyes and talks to her baby.*)

MARTHA. I'm sorry you won't get to taste a warm drop of milk…or swing on a rope swing…or feel that feeling of a first sweet bittersweet kiss when the person you've dreamt of fills you with moisture and warmth. And most of all, I'm so sorry that I won't get to meet you. *(changing tone slightly)* But I cannot emphasize enough how much easier this would be if you'd just stop moving down there. Your mother's not feeling too stable right now, so would you stop kicking and let me go?

AMBROSE. And her child said:

MARTHA. *(the baby has stopped "kicking")* Thank you.

> *(Then, to the theatre:)*
>
> I took a deep breath –
>
> *(The* **MEN** *all inhale…)*
>
> And then, sudden as a shot –
>
> *(***PRIMBODY** *fires his old-timey pistol – BANG!)*

MARTHA. *(cont.)* – my water broke.

ALL MEN. *(softly)* Wooosh.

MARTHA. Just like that. I had about 150 years of contractions stored up, so once that ocean inside me came busting clean through – I bled and I bled and I bled and I bled…

> *(She reaches into her dress, into her "womb" and pulls out red ribbons of cloth, which the* **MEN** *gather in their hands, pulling and pulling, as* **MARTHA** *travels upstage…it's a beautiful moment, supported by music. The* **MEN** *exit with the red ribbons, as:)*

MARTHA. *(cont.)* They say when you die, you feel like you're falling and falling as if through a tunnel, and then you see light. Maybe you're in heaven. Maybe you're a cow. Or maybe, just maybe…you're a baby.

> *(***PRIMBODY** *brings on a simple wooden rocking chair.* **MARTHA** *sits in it. He gently covers her lap with a blanket.)*
>
> *(Then a* **DOCTOR***, played by* **AMBROSE***, enters dressed in contemporary surgical scrubs, and carefully hands* **MARTHA** *a baby. The newborn's swaddling cloth is made of an American flag.)*

DOCTOR. Nine pounds, ten ounces.

MARTHA. Thank you, doc.

> *(to the theatre:)*
>
> Look at her. Look at her…! Oh, Jesus God Buddha Moses Krishna Mohammed, would you look at my kid??

(beaming with pride)

MARTHA. I feel as if the entire universe throughout all of time has conspired to bring forth this potentially perfect new person from me. I want to sing to her; I want to dance with her; I want the whole world to just sit up and shape up and learn from my baby. This kid can't read and write yet, but she is an absolute genius. We've only just met, and she's already taught me the point isn't to *be* loved – it's *to* love.

(to the baby)

Isn't that right, little girl? The only safe place for you is with me.

(DOCTOR *re-enters with a medical chart.)*

DOCTOR. Martha, we got your baby's lab results back, and they're a little concerning.

MARTHA. Why?

DOCTOR. Your baby is an exact genetic match to you. And that's just not scientifically possible.

MARTHA. Of course it is. I raised myself. I've got every right to give birth to myself. I've been in a state of continuous expectation my entire life.

DOCTOR. What are you naming this child?

MARTHA. Mary. Mary Martha. Just like my mother, Pa.

(He gives her a strange smile, and then exits. **MARTHA** *is alone on stage in her rocking chair with her baby. She looks at it, and sings softly:)*

MINE EYES HAVE SEEN THE GLORY
OF THE COMING OF YOUR BIRTH.

(The **MEN** *filter back on during the verse below, dressed in period costumes – except for* **DOCTOR***. They sing a cappella:)*

MEN & MARTHA.

WE HAVE TRAMPLED DOWN THIS COUNTRYSIDE
AND FOUGHT FOR ALL IT'S WORTH...

(growing stronger)

MEN & MARTHA.

WE HAVE LOOSED THE MIGHTY VENGEANCE

OF A NINE POUND TEN OUNCE BABE.

HER TRUTH IS MARCHING ON.

GLORY GLORY HALLELUJAH

GLORY GLORY HALLELUJAH.

*(And **MARTHA** sings to her baby, alone.)*

MARTHA.

GLORY GLORY, YOU'RE THE PRETTIEST

GIRL ON EARTH...

(taking us out perfectly)

YOUR TRUTH IS MARCHING ON.

(Lights slowly fade on Mother and Child. Curtain.)

End of Play

Also by
Jim Leonard...

Anatomy of Gray

Crow and Weasel

The Diviners

V and V Only

OTHER TITLES AVAILABLE FROM SAMUEL FRENCH

CROW AND WEASEL

Adapted by Jim Leonard
from the Novel by Barry Lopez

A Mythical Play with Music Accompaniment / 5-6m, 3-4f / Unit Set

Crow and Weasel premiered at the Children's Theater Company of Minneapolis. Set in a mythical time when the world was new, it tells of two Animal People who travel to the Land Where Dreaming Begins. A coming of age story rich with implications for the way we live, it is a show for the whole family.

"A rare work: simple yet complex, familiar yet different, entertaining yet instructional...An entrancing piece of theatre, rich with message, color and universality."
– *Minneapolis Star Tribune*

"Utterly captivating."
– *Skyway News*

"If I were a kid today, I suspect *Crow and Weasel*...would be on my list of favorite [stories]."
– Minnesota Public Radio

OTHER TITLES AVAILABLE FROM SAMUEL FRENCH

THE DIVINERS

Jim Leonard

Drama / 6m, 5f / Unit Set

Winner of the American College Theatre Festival, this marvelously theatrical play is the story of a disturbed young man and his friendship with a disenchanted preacher in southern Indiana in the early 1930s. When the boy was young he almost drowned. This trauma and the loss of his mother in the same accident has left him deathly afraid of water. The preacher, set on breaking away from a long line of Kentucky family preachers, is determined not to do what he does best. He works as a mechanic for the boy's father. The town doesn't have a preacher and the women try to persuade him to preach while he tries to persuade the child to wash. When the preacher finally gets the boy in the river and is washing him, the townspeople mistake the scene for a baptism. They descend on the event and, in the confusion, the boy drowns.

"A splendid drama by a playwright...with poetic as well as human feeling."
– *Variety*

"*The Diviners*, which would be meritorious from anyone, is astounding from so young a writer...Renders the humor and horror of the hinterlands with staggering accuracy...Compelling."
– *New York Magazine*

Breinigsville, PA USA
18 March 2011
257940BV00006B/3/P